Sister Theresa came right out with it.

"Father, I hope you're not thinking of keeping the child here, because we can't."

"Why can't we?" asked Father Alberto pointedly. It would be a wonderful experience to have a child at the mission, even if it couldn't last for long, and living at Notaheng was certainly better than living in a South African orphanage.

For a moment Sister Theresa sat looking at Father Alberto in shocked silence, as though she already knew what was on his mind. "To begin with, Father," she said seriously, "this is a black mission, and—"

"Why, Sister, I'm surprised at you," Father Alberto interrupted. "Surely you believe that all children are God's children."

"Yes, of course," Sister Theresa answered drily. "But the child is white."

forever young, forever free

Hettie Jones

Based on the photoplay
written by Ashley Lazarus

A BERKLEY MEDALLION BOOK
published by
BERKLEY PUBLISHING CORPORATION

1

The truck inched forward, skidded, then stuck again in the slush. Andries cursed under his breath. Letting the motor idle, he glanced into the rearview mirror. A few yards back he could see Anna, huddled in her thin shawl, shaking the snow out of her broken shoes. Behind her, still struggling up the hill with the baby tied on her back, was the old woman, Nkhono. Nkhono had no shoes at all. Andries knew that the water was soaking through the rags on her feet. He felt guilty that he had made them get out to lighten the load. It hadn't made much difference; even without their weight the truck was overloaded.

Andries turned away from the mirror and looked ahead. The road curved uphill for about fifty yards and then disappeared. To his right the dripping mountains rose almost straight up, and bare patches of black rock glistened through the melting snow and ice. To the left of the road, which was unfenced, the land fell off sharply downhill into a deep ravine. Andries decided to back down the hill and drive up again. He shifted into reverse and lifted his foot very slowly off the clutch. The motor ground, strained almost to bursting; then suddenly the back wheels spun wildly, spewing mud everywhere. But the truck only sank deeper, almost up to the back axle.

Shivering, Anna looked at the boxes piled in the back and wondered what they could unload. They had left everything that could be left at Kimberley; the stove, their bed, Andries' tools—all those would be needed in Durban. If they ever got there, she thought suddenly! The snow was melting so fast it threatened to flood the road before they could get through the pass. They should never have tried to cross the Drakensberg at the end of winter, but there had been no help for it; they'd had to leave.

Anna looked at the tool box stenciled *Andries Pienaar, Digger, Claim #1075, Kimberley,* and at the diamond sifter lashed beside it. The diggings at the Kimberley mine had yielded nothing; now their claim had run out, they were broke, and the baby was hungry. They had to get to Durban and find work. Anna turned to Nkhono and the baby. The old woman looked so tired, but she had insisted on carrying Jannie.

Andries carefully shifted gear and again stepped on the gas. The back wheels spun once, then caught. But as the truck lurched forward, the icy road beneath it cracked and the ground began to fall away into the ravine, slowly at first and then faster. Andries stuck his head out of the cab and looked back in terror. It seemed as if a river had erupted beneath him and that the truck was swimming in the middle of it.

The icy river of mud swirled around Anna's legs. "Andries!" she screamed and tried to run toward the truck. "Andries!"

Desperately Andries tried to reverse, but in the mirror he could see Anna coming toward him. "Terug!" he yelled. "Terug! Anna! Get back!"

But it was too late. By the time Anna reached the truck, the ground beneath it gave way entirely. Leaning out, Andries just managed to clutch his wife's arm before they were swept upward as though lifted by some giant hand, and then allowed to fall. In terrifying slow motion the truck somersaulted into the ravine, spewing its contents in all directions, the sounds of its destruction mingling with Anna and Andries Piennar's dying screams.

Very slowly, Nkhono opened her eyes. Barely ten feet in front of her the land ended abruptly, with empty, echoing space where the road had been. She walked cautiously to the edge of the precipice and looked down. Only ice and snow and jagged rock were visible; nothing moved. Far below in the ravine what remained of the truck and the Pienaars lay buried forever under the fallen mountain.

In the silence Jannie began to whimper, and for a moment Nkhono swayed dizzily, as though ready to give them both up to the same fate. But then some deeper instinct, some abiding concern for the child held her, and turning away from the tragedy she started down the road to look for another way across the mountains. She had only a vague idea of where she was, but she knew that the Pienaars had been on their way from Kimberley to Durban on the coast. That meant Lesotho would be somewhere in between. Nkhono had been born in Lesotho.

The sky darkened, the melting snow slowed, stopped, iced over. The soaked rags froze to Nkhono's feet, bled, and then froze again. All night she made her way across the mountains, bent under the weight of the child on her back. The wind was bitter. Jannie woke up now and then, crying because he was hungry, but the cold made him too weak to cry for long. Nkhono fell several times and thought she wouldn't be able to get up again; weakened by hunger and hard work, at fifty she was no longer strong. Only her tremendous will kept her going. Sometimes she followed roads or the polestar, but she trusted only her instinct, only an unshaken faith that because she had been born in Lesotho, somehow she would get back there.

Just before dawn she descended past the snow

line onto a barren plateau and found a road that led into the foothills. She stopped and looked ahead, catching her breath. About a mile or so further on she could see an isolated group of buildings, but she kept fainting and didn't think she could get there. Barely able to stand, she dragged herself along until she reached the first house. On her hands and knees she crawled across the wooden porch to the front door.

No one was awake. In the dawn stillness, Nkhono heard only the harsh rattle of her own breath. Painfully she untied the blanket, wrapped it around Jannie, and lay him against the doorway. Then somehow she got to her feet, found the metal doorbell handle, and pulled it. Inside, a muffled bell struck and echoed. Nkhono slumped against the door, then collapsed beside the child on the frosted-over boards of the porch.

In her bare room at the back of the Nohateng Mission, Sister Theresa Marguerita sat up in bed. She had been dreaming of going to church in Ireland and at first thought the bell was part of the service, and that it hadn't really rung at dawn in Nohateng. But a certain metallic echo coming from the hallway convinced her she'd better get up and check.

She groped around in the dark for her habit, which she had left at the foot of the bed. During the winter it was always very cold in her room at night, and by the time she had struggled to pull the habit over her nightgown, she was freezing and furious. "Blessed Mary, who'd be waking the

Lord's holy servants at such a God unearthly hour," she muttered. "Ain't the night sacred no more?" Angrily she slammed the door of her room behind her, and stumbling along in the too large woolen socks she always wore to bed, she crossed through the dark hallway to the kitchen and slammed the kitchen door too.

At the front door she put her ear to the keyhole and listened, while trying unsuccessfully to hike up her nightgown under the habit and at the same time to pull the habit down over her bedsocks. But there wasn't a sound from outside and the bell didn't ring again. Sister Theresa pushed aside the curtain at the small window in the door, and raising the candle, peered out. She couldn't see a thing except the empty porch rails silhouetted against the greying sky. "Blessed Mary and St. Patrick, there's probably nobody there, but I might as well see," she sighed. She swung open the heavy wooden door, shuddering as the freezing night air hit her.

Nkhono's twisted body fell across the sill. "God above!" Sister Theresa gasped. She knelt down, holding the candle to the old woman's face to see who it was, and was astonished to see a stranger.

Nkhono opened her eyes. Painfully, she raised her head and whispered through her torn lips. *"Lebitso ... lebitso ...."* She lifted her hand and tried to point to the blanket beside her.

Sister Theresa leaned closer. The woman was speaking Sotho. *"Lebitso ... la ... ngoana ke ... Jannie,"* Nkhono whispered. Then her head fell to one side, her frozen hand dropped lifelessly onto the blanket.

Confused, Sister Theresa repeated the old woman's words. *"Lebitso ... ngoana ... ke ...* the name of the child is—Jannie." Then, remembering the woman's gesture, she moved the candle nearer the blanket and with trembling fingers slowly pulled one corner of it aside. The child was about three years old and very pale, but he was alive. "In the name of the Father and of the Son and of the Holy Ghost," Sister Theresa gasped, crossing herself hastily. Gathering child and blanket in her arms, she fled down the hall to wake Father Alberto.

Father Alberto Assisi de Jesus was in a deep sleep. But when the knocking and shouting began, he sat up in bed, terrified. The knocking continued. All at once he became aware of Sister Theresa's urgent cries for him to get up. He stumbled out of bed and opened the door, unable to sort out dream and reality.

Sister Theresa turned her back on this very worldly sight of a sleepy man in his long winter underwear and started down the hall to her room for more blankets. "Hurry and get the stove goin'!" she called over her shoulder. "A strange woman brought a baby and then died on the doorstep!"

Father Alberto didn't believe a word she said, but he found his robe and slippers and stumbled into the kitchen, totally confused and disoriented. He threw a huge pile of wood into the stove and used a newspaper he hadn't even read to start the fire. He was standing and watching the words burn up when Sister Theresa came into the kitchen and sat down in front of the stove with a child on her lap. "Warm up some milk," she ordered Father Alberto, who had transferred his anxious stare to the shivering child. But then she changed her mind. "No, you're too slow, let me do it." she said. "You're half asleep and there's a baby boy here freezin' to death."

Relieved, Father Alberto took the child from her and sat down, unable to comprehend that someone had managed to bring a baby to his doorstep in a virtually inaccessible mountain village in August, the middle of winter. It was truly amazing. Perhaps it was a miracle. He stared at the child and touched his cheek gently. The little boy's pale skin appeared almost blue. His thin body felt stiff. He looked terrified, but he wasn't crying.

Sister Theresa bent over and put a glass to the child's lips. He drank the milk slowly, gasping a little, his blue eyes staring over the rim of the glass. "Where's your mama, Jannie?" she asked. When the child didn't respond, she asked him the same question in Afrikaans.

Jannie looked at her a moment longer, then burst into tears, turned away, and hid his face in the blanket. At this Father Alberto woke up and asserted his authority as head of the mission. "We'll ask him questions later, Sister," he said, patting the child. "Right now let's just feed him and put him to bed."

"I was just trying to help him," Sister Theresa said archly.

But she did as he suggested and put Jannie in her bed under a lot of blankets and sat beside him until at last he stopped shivering and fell asleep. Then she got up to dress, considering what they ought to do with him. No doubt someone will claim him, she said to herself. . . . But surely he can't stay here, it wouldn't be right. After some further thought she decided that they ought to leave the matter to the Archbishop in Maseru. Sister Theresa was the soul of caution, a virtue that drove Father Alberto crazy.

She buttoned her habit and adjusted her wimple, hoping that Father Alberto would feel the same way as she did about the child, though she could never be sure. Even after living and working together for ten years, they had never really become friends. They maintained at best only an uneasy peace. Sister Theresa had come to the mission from Belfast, where she had taught school. But she had left Ireland because, although a patriot, she could not bear the fighting, and also in the world of cities everything happened too fast for her. She had come to Nohateng to find peace and to teach as she felt was proper: toe the line, say your times tables in the corner and your prayers at bedtime. She had been thirty when she came and as rigid in her principles as she was devout in her prayers. She had taken over the running of the mission and the school it maintained from an old priest, who was glad to let her take the responsibility he no longer wanted. For five years she had ruled with an iron hand, having her own dogmatic way about everything. Then the old priest had died, and Father Alberto was assigned to Nohateng as head of the mission. He turned out to be exactly her opposite. Although they might have complemented each other, neither could adjust, and they were invariably at odds. In the matter of dress, for one instance, Sister Theresa preferred to wear, winter and summer, the old voluminous white habit that nuns in her order had put aside nearly a decade before. She tripped all the time, had difficuly climbing up the path to the village, and was always dusty at the hem, but she steadfastly refused to wear anything else. Father Alberto, on the other hand, wore khaki pants and boots, except when he performed ceremonies, at which time he put a robe over his usual clothing. Whenever she complained about his appearance, he would refer her to some verse from the Bible, or ask her whether she thought the Lord minded as long as he was doing his work, or some such irreverent answer.

With a sigh Sister Theresa looked at her watch and then hurriedly drew the plain muslin curtain across the window. The sun was already stream-ing in. Soon the village children would be coming to the one-room schoolhouse across the court-yard. In the darkened room Jannie appeared to be sleeping peacefully. So she gathered her books, shut the door quietly behind her, and went to her class. At intervals during the morning she looked in on him. Amazed to find him still asleep, she checked several times to see if he was breathing. It wasn't until two in the afternoon that she found him sitting up in bed in his dirty wrinkled clothing, dazed but far less pale, his blond hair askew. There were tears in his eyes and his lower lip trembled. Overwhelmed with pity, she picked him up, wondering what he had been through, and held him close in a genuine maternal gesture that wasn't characteristic of her. Sister Theresa was usually stiff and not very affectionate.

But it wouldn't do to get too attached to the child, she reminded herself. With few efforts at communication, she gave him a warm bath in the kitchen sink and dressed him in some clean clothes she had borrowed from a family in the village. And she fed him some more milk and as much bread and butter as he would eat. Then, taking him by the hand, she led him into the study to confer with Father Alberto.

Late afternoon sun slanted into the room, which like the other rooms in the mission house was bare of furniture except for a desk and a few chairs. But Father Alberto had a fire going against the chill, which made the winter afternoon more cheerful. In the morning he had tended to the burial of the old woman, whom none of the residents of Nohateng had recognized. He had prayed at her grave, humble and saddened as always at the presence of death, but trusting to God that she had wanted to come to Lesotho. But then in the afternoon he had taught school and his class had done well. He had come back to his study feeling proud and optimistic, grateful that he had been able to find a reasonably satisfying life. He was sitting at his desk now, feeling pretty good.

It could have been very different, he thought, tilting his chair back and watching as the flames curled around the logs. He might have had to remain in the cities that had distracted him so... New York, where he was born, Paris, Madrid. Before he had come to Nohateng he had tried at least three different places where he could work as a priest, helping and teaching people. But each time his offbeat principles had thrown him into conflict with established authorities. Finally, in a desperate move to try one more time or quit, he had come to Nohateng, where, with only Sister Theresa to reckon with, he had settled willingly into a life of hard work and service.

When he looked up and saw Sister Theresa in the doorway he thought he might even be able to count her as a blessing one day, for though strict, she was a good teacher and really wanted her students to learn, as he did. But there was something on her mind, he noticed. He could tell by the way she came in and sat down on the edge of her chair. The child at her side seemed withdrawn and confused. Father Alberto hadn't had time to give his presence much thought, but now that he looked at Jannie he realized he needed to consider what they ought to do about him.

Ignoring Sister Theresa's problem for a moment, Father Alberto picked Jannie up and sat him in a chair by the window. Then he produced from his desk a red lollipop. Jannie accepted it solemnly, but made no attempt to eat it. Father Alberto smiled at him and then, still smiling, turned to Sister Theresa.

She came right out with it. "Father, I hope you're not thinking of keeping the child here, because we can't."

Her use of "can't" immediately set Father Alberto's brain racing in the opposite direction. "Why *can't* we?" he asked pointedly. He sat down at his desk, ready to fight. It might be a wonderful experience to have a child, even for a while, he thought, for he was quite sure someone would claim Jannie soon enough. Meanwhile there was an extra room he could have. Living at Nohateng was certainly better than living in an orphanage, especially in South Africa, where the authorities would probably put him.

For a moment Sister Theresa sat looking at Father Alberto in shocked silence, as though she already knew what was on his mind. "To begin, Father," she said seriously, "this is a black mission, and—"

"Why Sister, I'm surprised at you," Father Alberto interrupted. "Surely you believe that all children are God's children."

13

"Yes, of course," Sister Theresa protested. "But the child is white."

"I noticed," Father Alberto said dryly.

"But if no one comes for him, he can't grow up here, in an all black village in the middle of nowhere in the Drakensberg mountains." Sister Theresa leaned forward and stared at him sternly. "More likely the child's from South Africa," she said in a tense, lowered voice, and if he has any family left they would *certainly* not want him to grow up here." She sat back and set her jaw in her fierce Irish expression.

Father Alberto tilted his chair back and looked down his nose at her while he mentally counted to ten. He found it unprofitable to stay angry with her and could usually talk himself out of it by this method. "Listen Sister," he said, speaking slowly and with more patience. "The child was left on our doorstep. The only person who could shed any light on who he might be is dead, and we haven't the faintest idea where he came from. So—" He paused to see if his message was getting through. But though he had thoroughly convinced himself, he hadn't been so successful with her.

"I think we should regard the child as an abandoned orphan," he went on, though a little less sure of himself. "As such it would be our duty to care for him. And until the Lord shows us another way—" here he looked up, properly reverent "—he'll be brought up here ... with all of us."

14

Sister Theresa stood up and walked to the window. Why can't he be reasonable? she thought. "Look outside, Father," she said. "That's Lesotho out there, not New York. Suppose they don't want a white child here?"

Father Alberto swallowed hard, trying to keep his temper. Why did she always have to expect the worst of people? "Sister," he said quietly, "It's 1968 now—and we're all out here together."

Sister Theresa knew from the expression on his face that there was nothing she could do, at least for the moment. She sniffed, gave him a hard look, and turned to go. "I'll have to see to the tea now," she said. "Will you mind him?"

"Sure," he said, glad to be delivered of her and pleased that the matter had been settled, though not quite sure what to do next. He watched Sister Theresa disappear down the hall and then looked at Jannie, who sat staring out the study window, still clutching the untouched lollipop. It would be like having a son for a while, Father Alberto thought. What an opportunity for a priest! To have a son without sin. He sat down on the arm of the chair and smiled at Jannie, feeling already totally devoted.

But the child looked away, his attention drawn to a commotion on the proch outside the window. Some of the children of Nohateng, having heard about Jannie's arrival, had come to look at him. Father Alberto opened the window and sat on the windowsill with Jannie on his lap. Everyone crowded around. "His name's Jannie," he explained to the children, "and he's going to live here with us for a while."

"Will he come to school, Father?" asked Willie, who was good in school and wanted to know if he was going to have any competition.

"Not yet," laughed Father Alberto. "When he gets older, yes. But he's too little now."

Suddenly the smallest child in the group, who was about the same age as Jannie, came forward and stood in front of the others, pressing up close against the windowsill. It was his clothing that Jannie was wearing. He gazed curiously at this stranger in his clothes (he had never seen a white child), and then with envy at the lollipop in Janie's hand.

Jannie stared back at him.

"That's Tsepo," said Father Alberto. "Tsepo means trust."

"Tsepo," repeated Jannie.

"Hey, he can talk!" cried Father Alberto.

Everyone laughed. The laughter relaxed Jannie somewhat. All of a sudden he extended his hand, offering the lollipop. "Tsepo," he said again.

With a shy look at Father Alberto, Tsepo reached out for his present. He grabbed it, flashed Jannie a quick smile, and was off the porch a second later, with the other children in hot pursuit. When they were gone, Jannie turned and smiled at Father Alberto. "Tsepo," he said again, in a small, pleased voice.

Father Alberto leaned down and planted a kiss

on the child's soft cheek. "I like your generosity, young man," he said, "and I think you've found yourself a friend." But as he sat beaming with pleasure at Jannie, a new concern rose to his mind. Jannie's people were no doubt from some place in South Africa—Afrikaners, probably not Catholic. To raise him a Catholic might in some strict sense be considered a sin. He looked at the boy thoughtfully, but although this new aspect complicated matters, to change his mind would have meant conceding defeat to Sister Theresa: something he would never, never do. So hoisting Jannie onto his back for a piggyback ride, he dispelled his misgivings and started down the hall. He hoped she hadn't been too angry to make them some toast with their tea.

2

   After Jannie's arrival, life went on much the same way at Nohateng. Sister Theresa taught school in the morning, cooked, cleaned, washed, sewed, and tutored in the afternoon, and prayed for everyone's soul in her free time. Father Alberto directed the village farm, greased, oiled, and swore at his old tractor in the mornings, and taught school, his primary interest, in the afternoon. Every Sunday he said Mass in the chapel for a few faithful followers, but he saw education, not conversion, as his duty. His religious beliefs horrified Sister Theresa. She considered him a renegade, if not a heretic, and threatened at least once a week to report him to the Archbishop—though so far she never had, because as well as being so sinful he was also an excellent teacher, farmer, mechanic, and handyman, all of which she appreciated.

In addition to the mission and the schoolhouse, the homes of the villagers and small patches of farmland that clung to the mountainside, Nohateng also sported a general store. The store was run by a fat genial man named Cash General, who owed his name to a sign (CASH—NO CREDIT) that he kept posted conspicuously on the door. Cash General and Father Alberto were close friends and joint owners of an old battered grey truck, Nohateng's only means of transportation to the outside world. Once a week their mail was delivered by plane, and Cash made monthly trips to Maseru, Lesotho's capital city, to get supplies. Occasionally Father Alberto would accompany him, but Sister Theresa never went anywhere, except to Ireland in her dreams.

No one ever claimed Jannie. He grew into a cheerful child, strong and athletic and good in school. He loved Father Alberto and tolerated Sister Theresa, but his favorite friend from the day of his arrival was Tsepo, and they were inseparable.

They ate fire-cooked goat's meat and 'mputu in Tsepo's house as well as oatmeal in the mission kitchen. In winter they slid down hills on sisal leaf sleds; in summer they played on a cable slide Father Alberto made them that went right through a waterfall into a mountain pool. Locomotion was their favorite game; they rode

Tsepo's father's goats and Cash General's donkeys, and went with Father Alberto in the old truck to get the mail. Following Cash and Father Alberto's example of joint ownership, Jannie and Tsepo together owned a dog, which they raised from a puppy and named Sugar Ball.

After her first attempt, Sister Theresa made no further moves to send Jannie away, for in her own way she loved him. But she had never been firmly convinced that they had done right in keeping him. After all, she reasoned, his family might be *somewhere*. And she was particularly upset because Father Alberto persistently refused to baptize the child. When Jannie was little, whenever she brought up the subject he would give her some evasive answer, and after a while she had stopped asking. Nevertheless she vowed that Jannie would learn his prayers. By the time he was nine he knew them well, although she still found it necessary to spy on him to make sure.

One moonlit spring night in November, he was on his knees beside his bed. He and Tsepo had been outside playing nearly all day long, and it was between yawns that Jannie recited: "Our Father who are in heaven, hallowed be thy name..."

He finished that and with a sigh began the required three Hail Marys: "...full of grace, the Lord is with thee..."

Those done, he rested his head on the covers and would have climbed into bed right then if he had not heard Sister Theresa's footsteps at the end of the hall. "Angel of God," he began again, with a big yawn, "my guardian dear, to whom God's love commits me here . . ."

A wave of sleepiness overcame him and his eyes closed momentarily. Something about the rhythm of the prayer reminded him of other words and he found himself saying, without even knowing what they meant: *"Liewe Jesus . . . sag eneer, sien my deur die donker nag . . ."*

Sister Theresa came to a stop outside the door, just in time to hear the unfamiliar prayer. "God in heaven," she said to herself, "he's praying in Afrikaans. His family must have taught him that long ago." That's why Father Alberto would never baptize him, she thought. She stood silently in the hall for a while longer, stunned by this new knowledge, but then habit won out. She stuck her head in the door and looked at Jannie, who was almost asleep on his knees. He looked like a little angel to her, and she wanted to rush in and embrace him, but she thought that would spoil him. "Have you said your prayers?" she asked sternly.

Jannie nodded.

"Well then, straight to bed." She slammed the door behind her, and Jannie heard the flap flap of her slippers going down the hall. He wondered why she was always so mean. She was mean not only to him, but to Tsepo and everybody, even Father Alberto. And she hardly ever talked to Cash General. He started to climb onto the b~ then hesitated and knelt down again. "Dear~

he prayed, shutting his eyes tight. "Dear God— please—you've got to do something about Sister Theresa!" Then he shook his head sadly and climbed into bed.

From time to time after overhearing Jannie's prayer, Sister Theresa thought about speaking to Father Alberto about it, but somehow, she didn't want to start anything. Yet along with her nagging guilt about the child's true religion was her belief that Jannie's upbringing had been far too permissive, due to Father Alberto's lenient nature. He was as bad as the Africans, she thought, who were all far too easy on their children. She began to think that in keeping Jannie they had done him a disservice.

He was misbehaving in school too. One day he and Tsepo threw erasers and devised a particularly nasty trick with a tin box that caused an uproar and completely disrupted the math lesson. She decided to keep them after school. After dismissing the rest of the class, she sat facing them, her habit a mess after the day's escapades. The boys sat side by side at the desk they shared, slightly ashamed but not very repentant. It was mid-December, and outside lovely and warm. They could hear Sugar Ball barking as the other children played with him in the courtyard.

Sister Theresa opened the drawer of her desk, took out the tin box, and put it on top of her books. "I've had enough of your tricks," she said, "and I'm thoroughly tired of you. Now go stand in your corners and be repeating your times tables till I come back." Taking books and tin, she huffed out, her dusty habit dragging like a broom over the hard packed earth of the schoolhouse floor.

Jannie and Tsepo watched her go, trying not to laugh. They had prepared another trick for her and couldn't wait for it to happen. But they dutifully walked to two separate corners of the room and began reciting: "Two times one is two, two times two is four..."

Suddenly from the nearby school outhouse came a piercing scream and then loud shouting. "Blessed Mary, St. Patrick, and the Lord!" Sister Theresa was yelling. "Get out! Out!"

Jannie and Tsepo ran to the back window. The door to the outhouse faced them across the yard and just as they looked out it burst open. A large green dripping wet bullfrog came hopping across the courtyard, croaking grumpily and dodging the books that were being thrown at him. Sister Theresa, whose shoes were on the floor, was standing on the toilet seat in her socks. Her habit was pulled up above her bony knees and she was clutching the tin box and throwing books. Tsepo turned away from the window and looked at Jannie, who collapsed onto one of the desks, his face beet red from laughing. "Two times three is six," he whooped, and they dashed back to their corners, still counting but mostly giggling.

After she collected herself, Sister Theresa went directly to Father Alberto's study and interrupted his only free hour of the day. He had his feet up on the desk and was reading peacefully when she burst in the door. "Father you'll have to do something...I...I just can't take them anymore," she said in one breath. She was so angry that she was near tears, but turned her back so that he wouldn't see. "They're uncivilized little demons, that's what they are," she said.

Father Alberto didn't know what had happened, but he was sure she would be over it soon, as usual, and also he wanted to read his book. "Come on, Sister," he said, patting her shoulder. "Don't take it so seriously. After all, they're only boys."

"Only boys!" Sister Theresa pulled away from him and slammed the tin box on his desk.

"What's that?" asked Father Alberto.

"Open it—go on, open it!" she shouted.

Gingerly, Father Alberot lifted the box, which was an old tea container. Turning it around, he opened the top. Instantly, the box erupted a spray of black ink all over his face and down the front of his oldest and favorite shirt. "Ach!" he yelled, spitting and searching for his handkerchief.

Sister Theresa allowed herself a smile. She was delighted to see him get some of the same treatment usually reserved for her. "Only boys," she said sarcastically, and stomped out of the room.

Father Alberto finished wiping his face and looked furiously at his ruined shirt. He acknowledged that he hadn't minded their tricks, as long as the tricks were on *her*. But this was really disgusting. There was a metallic taste of ink in his mouth. Ugh—this had to stop, really.

When he arrived in the schoolhouse, his face still streaked with ink and his shirt sodden, Jannie and Tsepo took one look and shrank back into their corners. Their ingenious device—an old inkwell, forced into an old car seat spring, forced into an old tea box—had obviously not been intended for him.

"Do you know what a spanking is?" he asked gravely.

They nodded, then prepared for the worst.

Sister Theresa went to her room and sat down on the bed. Don't take it so seriously! Only boys! she said to herself. No, he's wrong. The time to be serious is *now,* before the child grows up completely undisciplined. I'll just have to report this. I should have done it long ago.

She got a piece of paper from her desk and began a letter, addressing it to the Archbishop in Maseru. "Dear Archbishop," she wrote firmly, "I am writing with regard to a white child being brought up in the mission at Nohateng..."

She went on to tell the story of Jannie's arrival and her own versus Father Alberto's opinions about the matter. She ended: "...therefore I believe it to be in the child's best interest that he be taken away from here immediately." She signed her name, addressed an envelope, and sealed it. It looked very official and very final. She thought of Jannie and immediately felt some misgivings. But she decided to send it anyway. "Lord forgive me," she said aloud. "I hope I'm doing the right thing."

Then she went outside and crossed the road. It was Friday, market day, and the store was busy. There were people sitting on benches outside and standing around inside. Cash General, puffing like a steam engine, was serving three customers at once, his baggy grey pants held up over his broad belly with barely elasticized suspenders. When Sister Theresa entered he didn't notice her until his wife, Mama Joy, poked him with her elbow. "Look who's here," she whispered. Sister Theresa usually stayed away from the store, because at night Cash sometimes ran a "shebeen," or illegal bar, and Sister Theresa listed alcohol as the eighth deadly sin.

She walked to the counter. Cash noticed that she was sweating and that her habit was dreadfully stained. "What can I do for you, Sister?" he asked.

"I wonder if you would mail this the next time you're in Maseru," she said primly, with a hint of a nervous smile.

"Er...yes, surely," Cash mumbled. He took the letter from her.

"Thank you," said Sister Theresa, and turning on her heel, she walked swiftly out the door and shut it firmly behind her.

Mama Joy came to look at the letter over Cash General's shoulder. "It's to the Archbishop," he said to her, his eyes widening. "I think I'd better show this to Father Alberto before I mail it."

After Jannie and Tsepo left the schoolroom they went right to the pool, stripped, and lowered their sore bottoms into the cool water. But though they swam for a while, the water wasn't enough of a cure. Jannie climbed up on the bank and touched his behind gingerly. It hurt.

"You still sore?" asked Tsepo.

Jannie nodded. His feelings were hurt as well. He never expected Father Alberto to hit them so hard.

Tsepo climbed up beside him and checked his own rear end. It was still a little sore too. They probably needed some medicine. He remembered that Rakwaba, Nohateng's witch doctor, had given him some medicine once for a sore arm, and that the pain had gone right away. He started to put on his clothes and then motioned for Jannie to get dressed too. "Come on, let's go," he said.

"Where to?" Jannie asked.

"To Rakwaba. He has good medicine for sores."

Jannie watched Tsepo dress, feeling doubtful and uneasy. Sister Theresa had forbidden him to have anything to do with Rakwaba, and he knew there was some bad feeling between Rakwaba and the mission, but he didn't know what. He put on his shirt and then dawdled, throwing stones into the clear spring water and watching them descend.

Tsepo looked at the sun. It was getting late. "Rakwaba will fix your sore bottom," he said. "But if you don't want to come it doesn't matter. I can go by myself." He started up the path.

Jannie hesitated, but only for a moment. He decided he didn't care what they said. He wanted to see Rakwaba for himself. He ran to catch up.

Tsepo led Jannie along a narrow path that continued past the round thatch and mud homes in the village and higher up onto the mountain that overlooked all of Nohateng. Almost at the top they came to Rakwaba's hut, which had been built between two large jagged black rocks. It was made of sticks and stones wedged with cattle dung and came to a point at the top.

Jannie stopped a few yards away and grabbed Tsepo's hand. On a tree in front of the hut sat two black ravens staring at them. On either side of the doorway hung dried bladders and oxtails.

Tsepo pulled at Jannie's hand. "You coming?"

Jannie nodded, took a deep breath, and followed Tsepo inside. For a moment neither could see anything except a small fire in the center of the hut. Then something was thrown into it and with a hiss the flames shot up high, revealing a heavyset old man, muscular rather than fat, with dark, compelling eyes. He was sitting on a rug at the back of the hut.

"Hello, Rakwaba," Tsepo said. "I brought Jannie."

"So I see." It was the first time he had ever seen the little white boy, although the village people had told him about Jannie, whom they called *ngoanaluti* (child of the mountains), and how he had come to Nohateng. But Rakwaba lived apart from the village and hadn't been to the mission in fifteen years. The old priest had driven him out then when a woman Rakwaba had treated died. So he had come to live on the mountain, and although the people of the village still came to him for medicine, he had nothing to do with Sister Theresa or Father Alberto. Cash General had told him Father Alberto was a good person, but Rakwaba refused to risk another confrontation. He sent word to Father Alberto that he was not interested in meeting him.

Rakwaba looked at his visitors for a long moment, rattling some small polished bones he held in his hand. Then he tossed them onto the rug, and after a glance at their position, he spoke, mixing English and Sotho: "The bones tell of evil... *le sebile na*. Have you been evil?"

Jannie and Tsepo both nodded.

"And *la shapua*? You've been punished?"

They nodded again. "By Father Alberto," Jannie added. He wanted to make sure the old man was clear about who had done it.

"Good," said Rakwaba.

Jannie looked confused.

"I say good," Rakwaba explained, "because a man must understand that evil deserves punishment before he becomes wise." Then he turned to Tsepo. "Where is your pain?" he asked.

Tsepo turned around and indicated his behind. Rakwaba looked at Jannie, who did the same.

"My medicine is strong," Rakwaba warned. "*Letla lefakang*. You will have to pay me."

Jannie looked at Tsepo. He had no money or means to get any.

"*Matto a bo mampharoane,*" Rakwaba said. "My payments can easily be obtained. I want only the legs of four lizards and the tail of a black scorpion."

"Oh," said Jannie, relieved. "We can get that."

"Good. Now turn around."

The boys did as they were told. Rakwaba reached for a dried ox bladder hanging on the wall behind him and applied some greasy medicine from it to each bare bottom. Then he carefully replaced the bladder on the wall and clapped his hands twice. "*Ho tla choachoasela,*" he warned. "It will sting for a while and then be better." Then he sat back and took up his bones. "Don't forget—*la lebala bo mampharoane*—lizard legs and scorpion tails—or the pain will come back."

"Yessir." Jannie and Tsepo pulled up their pants and hurried outside.

Watching them leave, Rakwaba laughed to himself. Tsepo had told him that the priest was always kind and gentle. They must have made him *really* angry, Rakwaba thought. The idea delighted him a great deal.

Jannie and Tsepo walked carefully along the path. It was getting dark and below them the houses of the village were barely visible. "Why doesn't Rakwaba like Father Alberto?" Jannie asked.

Tsepo thought for a moment and then pointed to his eyes. "They don't *see* the same," he said.

Jannie wasn't sure he understood. "Sister

Theresa says Rakwaba doesn't believe in God."
He was puzzled about that. "Why not?"

"*Sehole*—stupid!" Tsepo said. "Because Rakwaba believes in his own God."

Just then they came to a flat grey rock where a
lizard sat, all but invisible in the grey light. Tsepo
made a grab for it, but the lizard darted away.

"*Sehole—tooe!*" Janie said. "Stupid to you
too!" He gave Tsepo a push on the shoulder and
then ran down the path, laughing. Tsepo chased
him. Their laughter echoed down the mountain in
the quiet evening.

The sun was already down when Father
Alberto went across the road to the store to get
some fuel for the generator. He felt guilty and
worried that Jannie was still out. He noticed that
Tsepo's father's goats were not yet in the kraal.
Bringing the goats down from the mountain was
Tsepo's job.

Father Alberto met Cash coming out the door.
"Have you seen Jannie or Tsepo?" he asked.

"No," Cash said. He handed Father Alberto
the key to the oil tank and they walked slowly to
the tank, which was out in back behind the store.
"I did see Sister Theresa this afternoon, though,"
Cash said. "She came into the store."

Father Alberto stared at him. "Into the store?"

Cash pulled the letter out of his pocket. "She
asked me to mail this for her the next time I went
to Maseru."

Father Alberto reached for the envelope. "It's
to the Archbishop," Cash warned gently.

"Oh." Father Alberto took the letter and

scowled at the neat handwriting. He put it into the pocket of his khaki pants and then stood looking thoughtfully at the mountains while the oil can filled. He was puzzled. Her anger this afternoon hadn't even impressed him. "I suppose she finally decided to report me," he said. "Though I don't know why."

Cash shrugged. "What will happen, do you think?"

Father Alberto laughed. "If the Archbishop transfers me, I'll send you a postcard. Here." He handed the key to Cash, and then patted his friend's shoulder. "Thanks," he added softly.

"Don't mention it." Cash walked Father Alberto around to the front of the store and then watched the priest cross the road and disappear behind the mission. Well, he thought, if the Archbishop takes him away, they'll have to send a saint to replace him. Cash didn't think anyone but a saint could contend with Sister Theresa. Shaking his head sadly, he turned and went into the store.

Father Alberto started the generator and then turned on the dim bulb in the generator shed. He sat down on an old wooden crate, drew out the letter and after turning it over a few times, opened it carefully. As he began to read, the worried look on his face changed to a broad grin, and when he had finished he leaned back against the rough wall of the shed, laughing quietly. Poor Sister Theresa Marguerita, he thought. Always equating mischief with savagery, and fun with sin. He admitted to himself that he had been angry too, especially about his beloved shirt. But he didn't see anything "uncivilized" about Jannie, who was bright and strong and, Father Alberto thought proudly, very intelligent. Where could they send him now, five years later? He wondered if she had even considered what might happen to the child if he were taken to Maseru. Well, he wouldn't let her send Jannie away now, any more than he would have five years before. He folded the letter in half and pushed it deep into his pocket. Then he unscrewed the bulb and in the darkness felt for the back door to the house.

When he got to the kitchen, Sister Theresa was setting the table. She glanced at him but then looked away and said nothing. She had changed her habit. "Is Jannie here?" he asked.

"No," she snapped. "Perhaps he's run away to protest our unjust treatment of him."

Father Alberto kept silent, but her sarcasm was not lost on him. She'd probably like Jannie to run away, he thought angrily; it would save the Archbishop some trouble. After checking the fire in the stove, he sat down at the table. Just then Jannie entered the room.

"You're late!" Sister Theresa exploded.

Jannie nodded and slid carefully into his chair, wincing when his sore bottom made contact with the hard wood. Father Alberto covered his face to keep from laughing, then used the opportunity to say grace.

"Where have you been?" Sister Theresa asked when the prayer was over.

"With Tsepo," Jannie mumbled, looking at his

plate. He couldn't decide whether or not to tell them the truth.

"Where?"

Jannie looked up at her and then glanced at Father Alberto. "I was with Tsepo," he said with exaggerated clarity. "And we went to see Rakwaba." Small and defiant, he sat waiting their reaction.

Sister Theresa's eyes widened. Suppose I had written *that* to the Archbishop, she thought! They'd come and get him in a minute if they knew we had allowed him to go to a witch doctor.

Father Alberto looked at Jannie curiously. "Why'd you go to Rakwaba?" he asked.

Jannie stared back. "To get medicine," he said, "for our sore bottoms."

Relieved, Father Alberto smiled. "Did it work?" he asked.

Jannie nodded, still angry. "Why doesn't Rakwaba like you?" he asked.

"Rakwaba's likes and dislikes need not concern you," Sister Theresa said icily. "Eat your food."

Father Alberto ignored her. He looked intently at Jannie and tried to give him a decent answer. "I think it's partly because we've never met," he said at last.

"Rakwaba doesn't believe in God," Sister Theresa said, as though that finished the conversation.

"Tsepo says he believes in a different God," Jannie said to her defensively. He turned to Father Alberto. "Do you like Rakwaba?"

Father Alberto grinned at him. "I might like Rakwaba if he let me," he said. "Now come on, eat."

Jannie smiled back at him, but then after a glance at Sister Theresa, who sat stone-faced, he went back to eating and they finished their meal in silence.

Tsepo hadn't brought the goats down. He stopped at the entrance to his house. He could smell the food inside and he knew they were already eating, but he gathered his courage and pushed aside the grass mat that hung in the doorway. His family was seated around the fire. His father looked at him for a moment, then asked: "*Lpili li sa le naheng?*"

Tsepo shook his head.

His father's expression didn't change. "*Tsa m'o di orosa*," he said quietly. "Go get them." He turned back to his food.

"But the child hasn't eaten," Tsepo's mother protested.

Tsepo's father regarded her calmly. A man of some authority, he didn't usually explain his decisions. "*O lokela ho ithuta*," he said. "The boy must learn."

Tsepo ducked through the hanging and went back outside. He climbed up the hill behind his house and then continued along the rocky path up the mountain. In the near darkness he managed to find the goats. He led them down toward the village kraal, where the herds were kept at night, next door to the store. The wind had come up and he shivered, feeling suddenly very cold and hungry too, hoping that Mohale, the kraal-keeper, wouldn't yell at him. Mohale was only eleven, but he was very ambitious and he hated Tsepo, for he felt that Tsepo received favors from the mission because he was Jannie's friend. Tsepo was afraid of him.

"You're a little late," Mohale said sarcastically, opening the gate to let him in.

"Sorry," Tsepo mumbled. He was staring at two strange men who stood outside the kraal, leaning on the fence. He had never seen them before. One of them had a bicycle spoke in his hand. "Who're they?" he asked.

Mohale grinned evilly. "Friends of mine," he said. "Now go on home."

Tsepo turned and ran. Mohale locked the gate behind him and joined his friends. They walked quickly up the road and knocked at the back door of the store. Cash was checking his receipts when he heard their knock. Taking an old kerosene table lamp, he went to the window and, recognizing Mohale, opened the door. "What's the matter?" he asked, thinking that perhaps the lock on the kraal had stuck again as it had a few nights before.

Mohale didn't answer. Instead he stood aside to let the two men pass through. They strode into the room and shut the door. Mohale remained outside.

Cash backed up and set down the lamp. Then he walked around behind the table and leaned against it, trying to look brave. He knew his visitors. One was Steve Mawanga, a gangster from Maseru, and the other was Steve's "Spokeman," so-called because of the sharpened bicycle spoke he carried, which he had been known to use. "What do you want?" Cash asked, holding on tight to the table edge. He was terrified of the spoke.

"I've come to visit you," Steve Mawanga said with a malicious grin. He poked a long thin finger across the table and into Cash General's belly, then passed by the table and walked through the connecting doorway into the front of the store.

Cash followed. "Why?" he asked. "I've paid you this month."

Steve Mawanga whirled around and slapped Cash on the face. "You've been speaking against me in Maseru," he hissed. "Even to black men."

Cash was not too frightened to hold his tongue. "Only to warn others," he said defiantly, holding his stinging cheek.

Steve Mawanga grabbed him by the suspenders. "You're not really against me, are you Cash?"

The Spokeman glided up to them and gently but firmly pressed the deadly weapon to Cash's throat, directly over his jugular vein. Cash tried not to tremble, for fear it would slip

Steve Mawanga let go of the suspenders suddenly and stepped back, taking a small leather pouch from his pocket. He dangled it in front of Cash's eyes, then opened the pouch and spilled its contents into his palm.

Cash stared. Mawanga was holding a handful

of uncut diamonds—thousands worth—and probably stolen. "I want *cash* for these 'cattle,' Mr. Cash," he said.

"Who did you steal them from?" Cash protested.

Mawanga laughed. "What do you care about that for?"

"I won't have anything to do with them if they're stolen."

"Be reasonable, Cash," said Mawanga. "You're a black man, I'm a black man. What do we need the white man for?"

"And how does your stealing help us Africans?" Cash retorted. "Do you give us back our treasures? No! You steal for yourself!"

Mawanga looked at Cash with undisguised hatred. "I want *cash*," he repeated. "You sell them—and for the highest price. And don't tell your white man friend." Then without warning he reached out and punched Cash in the stomach hard. As Cash staggered backward, the Spokeman punched him in the eye.

Gasping for breath, Cash sank to his knees. The Spokeman pranced around him, laughing softly. Steve Mawanga bent down and pushed his fist under Cash's chin, forcing him back until he fell to the floor. Then Mawanga lowered the pouch of diamonds onto his chest. "Sell them, Cash," he said, "and sell them high."

Nearly unconscious from the pain, Cash didn't reply.

"That's better," said Steve Mawanga. "I like a

man who agrees with me." He nodded to the Spokeman, who opened the door. "See you, Cash," he whispered. Then, at a signal from Mohale, they shut the door quietly behind them and walked down the road to where their bicycles were hidden.

3

The next morning at sunrise the mail plane flew over and dipped its wings. Yawning, Father Alberto climbed into the truck, which as usual was parked in the yard next to the store. There was no sign of activity in the store or around it. "Cash is late, he must have had a big night," Father Alberto chuckled, although he hadn't heard any sounds of a shebeen the night before. He started the truck and then drove slowly past the kraal on his way to the landing strip, waving at Mohale, who was just unlocking the gate. He passed too quickly to notice Mohale's sneer.

Mohale felt drunk with success. He had money in his pocket for playing lookout the night before. And with Steve Mawanga as his mentor he felt he couldn't go wrong. By the time Tsepo's father came to milk the goats, he had planned a rich future as a gangster.

After his father left, Tsepo arrived to carry the buckets of milk to the mission kitchen. Mohale was drinking from one of them. Tsepo dropped his schoolbag and ran to the gate. "Stop, Mohale!" he called. "That milk is for the mission."

Mohale looked at him over the edge of the bucket and then slowly lowered it. "I don't care about the mission," he said grandly. "I don't need them." He would have bragged about Steve Mawanga had he not been sworn to secrecy. But just to be sure Tsepo understood who was boss, he took another drink from the bucket.

Tsepo opened the gate and went into the kraal. He didn't want to tangle with Mohale. It was getting late and he had on clean clothes. "Why are you picking a fight with me?" he demanded.

Mohale sneered. "Because you're always sticking up for the mission and *le ngoana kelhooa*," he said. "You're always playing with the white boy."

"*Habane ke motsalle oaka*—he's my friend!" Tsepo shouted.

"Well, this is what I think of your friend!" Mohale yelled back, and, raising the bucket, he threw the last of the milk in Tsepo's face and then ran out of the kraal, laughing.

Tsepo, biting his lip to hold back the tears, picked up the empty bucket and leaned it against the kraal fence. Then he wiped his face, took the remaining bucket and his schoolbag, and walked across the road to the mission. He hoped Sister Theresa wouldn't yell at him too much.

When he returned with the mail, Father Alberto parked the truck beside the store and went back to the mission. He thought it was strange that there was still no sign of Cash. He took the mail to his study, where Sister Theresa was waiting to see it before going to her class. There was a registered letter in the pile. Father Alberto picked it out and turned it over, watching Sister Theresa out of the corner of his eye. She appeared to be still in a terrible mood. He slit open the envelope.

"Well, what's it about?" she asked, jumping up and trying to read the letter over his shoulder.

"Patience, Sister," he said, waving her back into her seat. The letter was from the United States. "In helping the underdeveloped nations of Africa," Father Alberto read aloud, "as part of our educational program we offer the services of our volunteer graduates. Pending your permission, we would assign to the Nohateng Mission Miss Carol Anne Duxley, a social science graduate of Wyoming State University."

"But who is it from?" Sister Theresa asked.

Father Alberto looked at the letterhead. "It's from the Peace Corps," he said.

Sister Theresa stood up, preparing to go. "Well, just write them and say no thanks," she said.

Father Alberto looked astonished. "But why?"

"Because first, we're not a charity case," Sister Theresa said firmly, "and second, we don't need her here."

"But Sister, why do you say that?" He was truly puzzled, since she was always complaining about having too much to do.

Sister Theresa finished gathering her books. "Because Duxley is a Protestant name and this is a Catholic mission."

Father Alberto took a deep breath and counted to ten. "Sister," he said finally, trying hard to keep his voice down. "Sister, I don't know what it is about Ireland, but—"

"What about Ireland?" she interrupted defensively. "It's a fine place."

"A fine place it may be," Father Alberto shouted. "But if everyone in Ireland is like you, no wonder they have such troubles!"

"Father!" Sister Theresa exploded.

Father Alberto ignored her and looked out the window where the children were gathering for school. "Anyone volunteering to help in Nohateng is welcome," he said. "We need help. If there is any problem it won't be because she's a Protestant, but because she's a woman. And that, my dear Sister Theresa—" He paused and turned to face her. "—that is something I sometimes think you have forgotten."

Sister Theresa stared at him in horror. "May the Lord forgive you, Father," she whispered.

"I think He understands," Father Alberto said serenely. While she stood dumbfounded, he gathered up Cash General's mail and that of the villagers, which he had sorted, and walked out of the room on his way to the store.

The store was still deserted. Father Alberto opened the front door, walked behind the counter and selected a paperback book from a pile on one of the shelves. All of the books were novels, glossy American paperbacks. Father Alberto pulled out from the pile of mail he was carrying a similar size book in a brown paper wrapper, and exchanged the book in the wrapper for the one he had just taken. Just as he reached to put the new book in his pocket, the door to the back room opened. Taken by surprise, he whirled around.

Cash General stood in the doorway, his one good eye staring at Father Alberto. "I see you're getting your weekly reading material," he joked.

Father Alberto stared. "What happened to you?" he asked. Cash's other eye was swollen shut.

Cash shook his head and motioned Father Alberto to speak very softly. Then he leaned against the counter and covered the swollen eye with a damp cloth.

"What happened?" Father Alberto whispered, handing him the mail.

"An accident," Cash General mumbled. He put the mail on the counter without looking at it.

"With whom?"

"Nobody."

Father Alberto was silent for a moment. "So, nobody did that to you?" he asked.

"That's right, a nobody." Cash turned away.

He was trying to obey Steve Mawanga's orders to keep his mouth shut.

Father Alberto got the hint. He walked to the window and looked out, then came back to the counter. "I need a new tire for the tractor," he said, willing to change the subject.

Cash turned his wet cloth on the cool side. "I'm going to Maseru Friday," he said. "I'll order it then."

"We've got a young woman from America coming to help at the mission," Father Alberto said enthusiastically.

Preoccupied with his wounds, Cash merely nodded. He didn't care who came to Nohateng from now on, as long as it wasn't Steve Mawanga.

Father Alberto took a closer look at the swollen eye. "You look like you need a drink," he said. He walked around behind the counter and pulled out from behind a sack of meal on the third shelf a half-full bottle of whiskey and a glass. He filled the glass, passed it to his friend, and watched while Cash took a slow sip of the drink. "It was Steve Mawanga, wasn't it?" Father Alberto asked quietly.

Cash looked at him. "*Ke molotsana noha e senang*," he said, a bitter edge to his voice. "He is a snake, *melemo ntle le chefu*—a snake that walks in the land."

Father Alberto looked grim. He clenched his fists and would have pounded on the counter had he not remembered Cash's sore head. Beside this problem, his own troubles with Sister Theresa seemed petty, easy to deal with, and decidedly unimportant. He walked to the front window of the store and stared out, feeling overwhelmed by everything he couldn't change. "It's time somebody put a stop to Mawanga," he said angrily.

"Stop him?" Cash shook his head. "*You* stop him, Father."

Across the road the school bell rang and the children came piling out of the classroom for recess, making their usual exuberant racket. Father Alberto's attention was drawn to a commotion in one corner of the yard, where Sugar Ball was growling and biting at something. Father Alberto left the store and sat down on the long wooden waiting bench outside. The growling across the road continued. Mohale had cornered Sugar Ball and was teasing him, trying to kick the dog with an old boot he had found in the yard and which he had put on over his bare foot. With a malicious grin, he kicked the dog and then stepped on his tail. Sugar Ball yelped in pain, unable to get away.

Father Alberto jumped up and would have run across the yard had not Cash come out at just that minute and held him back. "Let the boys take care of it," he cautioned quietly, indicating Jannie and Tsepo, who had just emerged from the schoolroom. He had a feeling that Father Alberto's intervention would just cause more trouble—and Mohale might call on Steve Mawanga to settle it. With a sigh Father Alberto sat down again.

Tsepo got to Mohale first. "Stop it!" he yelled.

"*Butle!*" Fists flailing, he dove at Mohale, but Mohale, who was much larger, grabbed him easily by the seat of his pants and swung him into the air. But while Mohale was dealing with Tsepo, Jannie snuck in. Crawling on his hands and knees, he pushed the boot off the dog's tail. Yelping, Sugar Ball fled.

Mohale let go of Tsepo and bent over Jannie, who was still on the ground. "And where do you think you're going?" he asked viciously, pushing his fist against Jannie's chin.

Jannie didn't answer. Although brought up never to fight dirty, he reached up and grabbed Mohale solidly by the crotch.

"*Moleko*—you bastard!" Mohale screamed and lashed out at Jannie, but he was too late. Before he could land a blow, Tsepo had bashed him in the face. Mohale staggered and went down.

But Jannie hadn't finished. He grabbed the boot and began to hit Mohale with it. Cash elbowed Father Alberto. "Time now," he said. "I think they've had enough." The two men walked quickly across the road and into the schoolyard.

Mohale's nose was bleeding all over his shirt, but he struggled to his feet, grabbed Jannie, and swung him into the air. "*Meha fatse,*" came the voice from behind them. "Put him down—right now!"

Mohale took one look at Father Alberto, released Jannie, and left as quickly as he could, holding his bloody shirt to his nose. Panting, the two boys turned to thank Father Alberto, but the

first thing they noticed was Cash General's
condition.

"Who did that?" Jannie asked, awed.

"A couple of Mohale's friends," said Cash.
"But next time I'll ask the two, of you for
assistance. You make a pretty good team."

Father Alberto answered the Peace Corps that
afternoon. Cash mailed the letter a few days later
when he drove to Maseru. As soon as the letter
was gone, Father Alberto began to have second
thoughts during the day and nightmares at night.
He came to the conclusion that he had done a
terrible thing. Worse, he had done it partly just to
win another battle in his ongoing conflict with
Sister Theresa. But though he doubted his ability
to handle the situation, he would never have
backed off. He knew he had to try and figured it
would be the Lord's test.

Sister Theresa prayed fervently, whenever she
could find the time, and tried not to let herself
think about Carol Anne Duxley. She felt he had
done it to spite her.

After several more letters with respect to time
and place, and several near arguments between
Father Alberto and Sister Theresa, they found
themselves one Saturday afternoon in January
waiting at the airstrip about five miles east of
Nohateng.

With everything arranged and the young
woman's arrival imminent, Father Alberto had
begun to feel extremely nervous. The night before

he even had a little nightcap before going to bed, thinking to relax. But instead he had slept fitfully for a while until he awakened in a cold sweat. Now he sat in the driver's seat of the truck, leaning his head against the cushions, trying to relax in the warm afternoon sun.

Jannie, who was sitting on the front hood, suddenly began to jump up and down, causing the truck to bounce and Father Alberto to rise in the seat and hit his head on the ceiling. "It's coming!" Jannie yelled. "I can see the plane."

The truck roof over Father Alberto's head thundered loudly as Tsepo, who had been sitting on it, slid across and down the front windshield to join Jannie. Holding his head, Father Alberto got out and went to stand with Sister Theresa and Cash General who had come along mostly out of curiosity, although he had insisted it was to help with the luggage. They watched as the plane, banking sharply, came down from the western range of mountains and then, sweeping low, headed for the barren brown strip.

With a few well-controlled bounces, the light plane came to a stop. Almost immediately the back hatch slid open. Carol Anne Duxley, after eyeing the three-foot jump, landed unevenly but upright on the ground and heaved a huge sigh of relief. It had been a long journey, and she was glad to touch ground.

The welcoming party approached a little hesitantly, somewhat mystified by what they saw, for to anyone outside the United States, Carol

Anne Duxley was quite a sight. She was carrying two firstaid kits slung over one shoulder and a camera over the other, but apart from that it was her clothing that was really astonishing to the residents of Nohateng. She wore tight blue jeans and a tee shirt, a pair of army surplus combat boots, and nothing else. Jannie and Tsepo noticed the boots first.

Father Alberto wanted to turn his back until this vision melted away. Nevertheless he stepped forward bravely. "Hello, Miss Duxley," he said. "I'm Father Alberto, and this is Sister Theresa."

Although Sister Theresa was in shock, she tried to remember her manners and reached out to shake Carol Anne's hand. "How do you do?" she said stiffly.

"Hi," Carol Anne said, obviously nervous too. Fumbling with her gear in order to extend a hand to Sister Theresa, she dropped one of the firstaid kits.

Father Alberto rushed gallantly to pick it up. "Thank you," she said, smiling at him when he handed it to her. He smiled back, a reaction not lost on Sister Theresa, who also noted that his eyes were beaming. Apart from her strange clothing, Carol Anne Duxley was quite attractive. She had short brown hair, a slim figure, and a pleasant expression on her face.

Father Alberto introduced her to Cash and the children, and everyone shook hands. "Oh, please, let me take a picture right away," said Carol Anne excitedly. "This is my first trip to Africa, you know. Here." She turned and handed the camera to Cash. It was a fancy, Polaroid camera, a type he had never seen.

"How do you work it?" Cash asked.

"It's easy." She showed him how to use it, and then stepped back into the group. "Now just lift it and press the button."

Cash fumbled. He lifted the camera with the lens facing him and, forgetting to turn it around, pressed the button. The flash went off full in his face, and he turned ashen as he jumped back, his first thought being that he had encountered a secret weapon from Steve Mawanga and would die.

Everyone laughed. "No no, the other way," Carol Anne said. She ran up to Cash, adjusted the camera and rolled the film, and then stepped back again beside Father Alberto. He smiled at her again. Slightly embarrassed but feeling drawn to him, Carol Anne smiled back just as Cash pressed the button.

Father Alberto tried to blink away the flash in his eyes. "H—have you any luggage?" he asked.

"Some," Carol Anne said.

Father Alberto went around to the other side of the plane and stopped dead. A mountain of boxes and suitcases lined the strip and more were being unloaded by the pilot, who was sweating and annoyed. "Can you help me with this, please?" he asked. "I'm due back in Maseru in half an hour."

"Cash, get the truck, we've got work to do," called Father Alberto. Curious, everyone else came round to see while Cash brought the truck from the end of the airstrip.

"Medical supplies," said Carol Anne to Sister Theresa, pointing to several large cases on the ground. "I've come prepared. And I've had shots for smallpox, yellow fever, bubonic plague, malaria, cholera, typhoid fever, and Asian flu. You don't have anything else here, do you?"

Sister Theresa was too overcome to reply. "No, I don't think so," put in Father Alberto, trying hard to suppress another smile. Suddenly Sister Theresa pointed to an object the pilot had just unloaded, that lay beside a sleeping bag and some tennis rackets.

"What's that?" she asked.

"Oh, that," Carol Anne answered. "It's a portable TV set."

"A TV set?" echoed Sister Theresa. "Why child, there's no TV here!" She looked down her nose, her tone decidedly condescending.

Carol Anne looked confused. "No television?"

Cash, who had overheard, leaned over the back of the truck. Contrary to Father Alberto, he was not shy with women, old or young. "Oh there's TV in Africa, but we can't get it up here in the mountains. If you don't find Nohateng enough of a show," he offered, "I'll take you to Maseru sometime." He winked at Father Alberto, who turned pale.

After the truck was loaded, Jannie and Tsepo jumped in and seated themselves on top of the crates, which promised a good ride home. Tsepo was disturbed by the fact that Carol Anne was wearing men's shoes. "*Keng ha a na le dieta tsa banna?*" he whispered in Jannie's ear.

"Oh, that's what they do," said Jannie wisely. "Everyone wears boots in America."

When they got back to the mission, after Cash and Father Alberto unloaded the truck and the boys went off to play, Sister Theresa took charge of Carol Anne. She was extremely irritated, not at the young woman's arrival, which she had already accepted as another burden in her already overburdened life, but at Carol Anne's apparent lack of modesty and the failure of U.S. officials in allowing her to arrive as nearly unclothed as an African. She hurried Carol Anne down the hall. "This will be your room," she said, "next to Jannie's." She ushered the young woman into the last room along the hallway, bare like all the others save for a narrow wooden bed, a few shelves and a chair. Carol Anne's paraphernalia was in a huge pile on the floor.

"Meals are served in the kitchen," Sister Theresa went on, anxious to point out the disadvantages of life in Nohateng. "Breakfast's at seven o'clock, lunch at 12:30, and supper at six. A woman from the village usually helps me out afternoons and now that you're here I'll expect you to help us with the cooking and the dishes, as well as any other duties we agree on later."

Carol Anne nodded seriously, but Sister Theresa didn't even look at her. "The bathroom is down the hall," she continued. "Hot water runs from 5:30 until 7 in the morning."

Carol Anne sat down on the bed, trying to take

it all in. Sister Theresa walked to the doorway, erect in her habit, which was again dusty, this time from the airstrip. "Oh, the lights," she remembered. "We generate our own electricity which is very expensive, so the lights are on only between six and ten in the evening. I trust that this will be sufficient for your needs," she ended primly. "Do you have any questions?"

Carol Anne looked at her in some confusion. "How come Jannie lives at the mission?" was all she could think of to ask.

Sister Theresa smiled at the question. "He was left with us, but he won't be here for long." She walked through the doorway and out into the hall, then remembering something else, stuck her head back in. "Tea's served at four," she said, her hand on the doorknob, and then slamming the door behind her, she rustled down the hall.

Carol Anne remained sitting on the bed for a few minutes. Then she swung her feet up and lay down, trying to sort everything out. But it was hard to do because she had been too excited to sleep on the plane and now she wasn't even sure what day it was, or what time. Her watch said eight o'clock, but whether that meant morning or evening she had no idea, and since it was obviously not Nohateng time, she unstrapped the watch from her wrist and decided to disregard it altogether.

"Probably only Sister Theresa knows Nohateng time," she said to herself, and then grinned at the ceiling. Sister Theresa reminded her of the nun she had had in first grade, when her father had insisted on sending her to a local Catholic school because of its scholastic reputation. He had removed her six months later because she continually disobeyed the rules. That had been in Nebraska, and she hadn't thought about it for many years, having lived and gone to school in so many places since then, hauled along as something of an afterthought to her father's political ambitions. And now still another home, she murmured, but at least this time I've chosen it for myself.

She got up, stretched and then touched her toes, found some gum to chew, and began to unpack. She set her cassette on the floor next to the bed and put on a tape. Familiar music always helped her to adjust to unfamiliar surroundings. When the first tape was over, she put on another and continued to unpack her sizable collection of jeans and tee shirts, with only every now and then a look out the window to remind herself that she was in Nohateng. She heard nothing but the music, though outside her room a certain amount of activity was going on too.

Jannie and Tsepo, having found a ready-made new victim, had decided to test her mettle. After a quick collection among the rocks and grasses on the mountain, they sneaked cautiously around the back of the schoolhouse and into the generator shed. Then inch by inch they opened the back door of the house, which was diagonally opposite the kitchen and faced the long hallway off which were the bedrooms. Sister Theresa was busy preparing tea and didn't see them. On tiptoe they went quickly to the last bedroom. Silently pulling a piece of string from his pocket, Jannie climbed on Tsepo's shoulders and Tsepo slowly straightened up. Carefully Jannie stuck a pin into the wood above the doorway and tied the string to it. This done, he climbed down. Tsepo then took from a tin box a live lizard, a particularly squirmy one, and tied it at face height in the center of the doorway. On the hallway floor in front of the door he put a small live snake, also from the box. As a final touch they also placed four dead lizards artfully around the snake, and when this was done they gave the hanging lizard a push so that it swung back and forth. Then they scrambled out the hallway window onto the porch and waited.

A few minutes later, Sister Theresa came out in the hall and rang the bell for tea. Carol Anne switched off her cassette. Without the music, she felt suddenly very aware of being in Africa, among strangers, in a bare old wooden room. Taking her watch from the shelf, she reset it to 4:00 P.M., thinking it might be a good idea to keep up with Sister Theresa's time. She opened the door, looking back over her shoulder at her progress in arranging the room, and then turning, walked full face into the squirming lizard.

Terrified, she screamed and ducked sideways onto the snake, which slithered onto her boot. Still screaming, she kicked out frantically, trying to get the snake off, but she slid over the dead lizards and fell against the door.

Sister Theresa burst out of the kitchen and came running down the hall, followed by Father Alberto, who had just come in to tea. "What is it, child? Why in the name of Mary, you're trembling like a leaf!" cried Sister Theresa, putting her arm around Carol Anne, forgetting her hostility for the moment at the sight of the young woman's ashen face.

Carol Anne shook her head wordlessly and pointed to the dangling lizard, which was still squirming, and then at the array on the floor. Sister Theresa shuddered and felt a flash of sympathy.

Father Alberto thought it was kind of a funny trick, but he felt sorry for Carol Anne, who seemed shaken and looked very tired. "It's nothing to worry about," he said. "it's only a *mampharoane*, a common rock lizard. It won't hurt you."

"I'll be wondering who put them there," Sister Theresa muttered.

"Now now, Sister," Father Alberto said. He untied the lizard and with a reassuring smile escorted both women back to the kitchen, feeling very chivalrous and grandiose. Outside on the porch, shaking with laughter, Jannie and Tsepo decided that even though they were hungry, it would be best not to go in for tea.

4

The next morning Carol Anne would have missed breakfast if Jannie hadn't knocked on her door. "Wake up Miss Duxley," he called through the keyhole. "Father Alberto says we can all go for a walk right after mass."

"OK," she mumbled sleepily, and stumbled out of bed, banging into things as she moved around the unfamiliar room in the pale early morning light. Outside her window, which opened onto the front porch, she could see the schoolhouse, and past that the road and the mountains. Even this early they looked hot. Carol Anne turned and crashed into the bed. She had come from a cold winter city in the northern hemisphere to midsummer in the mountains in the southern.

Even her body and sense of direction seemed resistant to the change, as though despite gravity she really felt upside down.

Sister Theresa was courteous but businesslike at breakfast. When Carol Anne stepped dutifully to the sink at the end of the meal without being asked, Sister Theresa was pleased and responded with a genuine, if distant, smile.

Several hours later, after Father Alberto had said Mass for his usual congregation of four, they began the grand tour of Nohateng. Sister Theresa didn't come along, partly because she had put on a clean habit for Mass. She watched them set off down the road. Father Alberto, like the girl, was wearing his usual faded pants. And on Sunday too. She shook her head sadly, feeling a wave of nostalgia for the rituals everyone had dutifully performed in the old days, like getting dressed up on Sunday. She hoped Father Alberto would at least leave his shirt on when walking in the village with the girl; he had been known to take it off when he got hot.

Jannie and Tsepo walked in front, the latter carrying as usual his tin box in case they came across some interesting specimens. Carol Anne watched them for a while, wondering about Jannie as she had the night before. "Father," she asked, "is Jannie going to live with his family?"

"Jannie's an orphan," Father Alberto said.

"Oh. Sister Theresa said he was leaving."

Father Alberto shook his head. "No, we adopted him." He said it with conviction, for he had come to believe it fully. He wondered what else Sister Theresa had told her about Jannie or about himself.

They crossed the main road on which the store and mission were located, and began to climb the winding rocky path that led up to the village. Father Alberto was pleased that although he set a fast pace, Carol Anne climbed easily in her combat boots and jeans and could keep up with him.

Jannie and Tsepo ran on ahead and soon disappeared. When they came to a level spot above the mission, Carol Anne looked down. "How long has it been here?" she asked.

Father Alberto launched into his favorite guided tour lecture. "Forty-five years," he said. "That is, as a Catholic mission. Before that it was a mission of the Anglican Church, but they gave it up because they made very few converts. The Sotho are a very independent people."

"I thought the Sotho were a tribe," said Carol Anne.

"That's a western concept," he said. "There's no word for tribe in any of the African languages. The word in Sotho is *sechaba-sa Basotho*—a people, or nation."

Carol Anne let this sink in while they continued on up the mountain. "It's very different from what I expected," she admitted shyly, a little out of breath from the climb. "I expected it to be greener, more trees, more like a jungle."

"You've been watching too much television,"

Father Alberto laughed. "No, the climate of southern Africa is dry except in the rainy season."

"You ought to be a professor," she said admiringly.

Father Alberto grinned at her sideways. He was still too shy to be able to look her straight in the eye.

They continued up the road in silence until they had reached the village, where they strolled among the houses, visiting. At that time of the year most of the men were down at the lower end of the village, working in the community farm, so Carol Anne met mostly women and children and old men, who were grinding corn and tying sheaves of thatch, for summer was also house repair time in Nohateng.

"Everyone's working," Carol Anne observed.

"Everyone has to work," Father Alberto said.

They climbed higher, beyond the village, until nothing obstructed their view of the stark dramatic peaks of the Drakensberg. Below them the rocky hillside slanted off into a sheer cliff, nearly three hundred feet high, below which coursed a narrow but swiftly running river. Beside the river ran a section of the narrow dirt road to Maseru. Far away to the left the mission buildings appeared tiny and brown, the way Carol Anne remembered seeing them from the airplane. "They call this 'the mountain that falls into the sky,'" Father Alberto said.

"It's almost like Nevada or the moon," Carol Anne said.

Father Alberto nodded. He had long ago ceased to compare Nohateng to any other place because it set up certain longings for other comparisons. He looked at Carol Anne, who was leaning against a ledge. She looked tired. "Let's rest," he said.

They sat down on a flat sun-warmed rock. Father Alberto gazed down at the tiny spot of the mission houses. "The Sotho call this place *mokokatlo oh lefatse*," he said. "That means 'the back of the world.'"

"Why would people want to live on the back of the world?" Carol Anne asked.

"The Sotho didn't always live in Lesotho, but they are a people with a fine spirit to survive," Father Alberto said, beginning another of his favorite lectures. "A few hundred years ago southern Africa was colonized by the Dutch and Germans and then by the English. The Zulu, who had been displaced, began fighting for land. About 150 years ago a Sotho chief named Moshesh, fleeing the Zulu chief Shaka, led his people into the safety of the mountains and they formed the Sotho nation. As Basutoland they were a British crown colony until they became independent in 1966 and changed their country's name to Lesotho."

"You're better than a textbook," grinned Carol Anne. "Or at least more up to date."

Father Alberto smiled at her and then looked away, flustered again. No one had complimented him so much, it seemed, for a long time.

Carol Anne looked at him, wondering how old he was. He didn't look old, except for his greying hair. "How long have you been here?" she asked.

Father Alberto stared at the mountains. "I guess about, well, almost twenty years." He knew that would seem like such a long time to her.

Suddenly Carol Anne felt sorry for him. "It must be lonely for you and Sister Theresa," she said.

But Father Alberto acknowledged only his sins, never his loneliness. "When you are close to God and his people, you are never lonely," he said, but he knew even as he said the words that it was a textbook sentence too. "Let's find the boys," he said quickly, and, jumping up, automatically offered his hand to Carol Anne.

Responding to his grasp she bounded up lightly and stood facing him. Father Alberto felt his face begin to go red, but he responded to her honest gaze with a very direct one of his own. They walked in silence from then on. Father Alberto concentrating on restoring his equilibrium, Carol Anne enjoying the sun and the scenery. "What's up there?" she asked when they got to the path that branched off toward Rakwaba's hut. One side of the hut was visible from where they were standing.

"That's where Rakwaba lives," Father Alberto said. "He's the witch doctor."

Carol Anne hesitated, obviously interested, but Father Alberto merely walked on ahead, making it very clear that they weren't stopping. "I have to get back," he mumbled over his shoulder." He knew she would find out about the conflict with Rakwaba in time.

Jannie and Tsepo had stopped at the point where the path crossed the village stream and were making clay figures on the bank. Tsepo started a rather large one and, working on it thoughtfully, suddenly asked: "Or-fan *keng*, Jannie? What's an orphan?" He had heard Father Alberto earlier on the road.

Jannie knew that one. Father Alberto had explained it to him once. "It's when you have no mother or father," he said.

Tsepo continued to model. "Father Alberto told Miss Duxley you were an orphan."

"Mmm," said Jannie, more concerned about the dog's body he was shaping.

"But you're not an orphan," Tsepo said.. "Father Alberto's your father and Sister Theresa's your mother."

Jannie stopped working. "No," he said. "Father Alberto told me I come from somewhere else, that an old woman brought me here when I was small."

"I don't believe it," said Tsepo.

"No, really," Jannie insisted. "And I know it's true because sometimes I think in another language—just like that."

"What language?" Tsepo asked skeptically.

Jannie hesitated, trying to remember. "*Sagen teer—hou my deur die donker nag*," he said slowly.

Tsepo wasn't convinced. "That doesn't even mean anything," he said. "Look—here's your mother." He lifted up his statue. It was an ugly clay figure of Sister Theresa.

"She's not!" yelled Jannie, outraged.

"Yes, she is," Tsepo teased.

"She's not!" Jannie was furious. He jumped up and smashed the figure out of Tsepo's hands. The wet clay crumbled into the stream.

Father Alberto came along the path just in time to see the last of the argument. "Hey, quit it!" he yelled. Then, turning to Carol Anne he said, "I'm due back at the mission. But the boys can look after you now and show you some more of Nohateng."

"OK," said Carol Anne. She watched his retreating back as he made his way along the dusty path. She was still wondering about the witch doctor.

The boys led her along the stream and then back onto the path up the mountain. "Where are we supposed to be going?" she asked after they had walked for a while. Her feet were becoming hot in the heavy shoes.

"Father Alberto said we should show you things," Jannie said.

"What things?"

Tsepo wrinkled his nose and winked at Jannie. "*Mampharoane le phepheng*," he giggled.

"Mampho what?" Carol Anne asked.

"Lizards and scorpions," Jannie snickered.

"Lizards and scorpions!"

"We have to get them for someone," he apologized, "but you can help us if you like."

Carol Anne looked shocked. She would have gone back to the mission right then, but she didn't know the way. With a big, engaging smile, Tsepo handed her his box, and she trailed them up the mountain while the boys caught various lizards, scorpions, and beetles, shoving them one by one into the box that she very reluctantly held. When it was nearly filled she had had enough. "Here, you take it now," she said, thrusting the box at Tsepo.

Reaching to take it, he suddenly froze. "*Che!*" he ordered, grabbing her arm. "Don't move."

Although Carol Anne wasn't used to being ordered around by nine-year-old boys, there was something in Tsepo's tone that made her obey. She stood motionless, following his example, trying to see what was wrong. There was something on the path in front of them, but it wasn't moving and appeared dead or inanimate, like a branch. She didn't understand what the fuss was about. But suddenly the inanimate branch whipped around, coiled, and rose into the air. What had appeared to be a harmless object became a deadly snake, Africa's spitting cobra, the band of white around its neck in stark contrast to its expanding black hood.

Carol Anne screamed and almost fainted with terror, but Tsepo's hand on her arm kept her still. The snake continued to move, its flicking tongue spitting deadly venom, its tiny beady eyes following their every move.

Neither of the boys showed any sign of fear. Jannie moved in slowly beside Carol Anne and then inch by inch crept along the path toward one side of the snake, shielding his eyes with his hand to protect himself from the venom. Tsepo pulled out of his back pocket his ketie, a slingshot made of a forked stick and a strip of old inner tube. Cautiously, his eyes still on the snake, he squatted down and after a quick search found a large stone, fit it into the ketie, and nodded at Jannie.

Jannie nodded back. "*Baleha!*" shrieked Tsepo, and at the same time Jannie dove, diverting the snake's attention toward himself. But as the snake struck out at Jannie, Tsepo let fly the ketie, and the sharp rock expertly, neatly, sheared off the top of its head. Jannie, leaping out of the way just in time, grabbed a large rock and smashed it across the writhing body. The snake twitched several times and then was still.

Carol Anne remained rooted to the spot, shaking. "It's dead now," Tsepo assured her, and to prove it, he picked up the long body and swung it gently by the tail. Then the two boys started up the path again. Carol Anne ran to keep up with them. She certainly didn't feel like being left alone. Tsepo continued to drag the snake's body behind him along the path.

"Wh—what are you going to do with it?" Carol Anne asked, after she had collected herself a bit.

"Jannie smiled cheerfully. "We'll give it to Rakwaba," he said.

"The witch doctor?"

Tsepo nodded. "We have to pay him," he said

gravely. "We owe him for some medicine he gave us once."

"Rakwaba doesn't believe in God," said Jannie. He thought she should know.

"Oh." Carol Anne stared at him. That would explain Father Alberto's refusal to take her to Rakwaba's hut. "But what does he believe in?" she asked, running to keep up with the agile boys, who climbed like goats among the rocks and ledges. There seemed to be a lot more to Nohateng than she had expected.

Rakwaba sat beside the ashes of his fire, his face impassive, staring at the trio that had come to visit him. Then he picked up the tin box that Tsepo had given him, lifted the lid, and looked at the writhing mass inside. "*Ke hantle bana baka*," he murmured with a satisfied nod. "You have done well." Then he set the box aside and stared at Carol Anne.

She was completely overwhelmed. The outside of the place had been incredible enough, with its weird things hanging everywhere, and now this old man. . . .

Rakwaba picked up his polished bones and rattled them, still looking at her thoughtfully. He had let her come in only because the boys had brought her, and because none of the white people he had ever encountered at the mission had expressed any interest in his beliefs. They had only tried to get him to accept theirs. "So you wish to know in what I believe?" he asked.

Carol Anne nodded and whispered an almost inaudible "yes."

"I believe in *Badimo*—the spirits of my ancestors—*ke bona ba buang*, for they speak," he said slowly. "And I believe in the power of the *Badimo*, for it lives—in the earth, in the sky—and inside us." He put his hand over his heart, and Carol Anne nodded, understanding.

Rakwaba's expression softened, almost, but not quite, into a smile. "But I am a doctor, you see," he went on, "so I believe in *litlhare*—the medicine of earth, in *metso ea lefatse*, the roots, leaves and bark of trees, in lizards and other crawling things, in the fat of lion and hippo—"

Rakwaba paused. "Those are strong medicines," he continued after a while, "but over all, I believe, is the power you cannot touch, for it is stronger than all."

Carol Anne was silent. Except for the lizards, it sounded like a perfectly acceptable religion to her. Actually she didn't know much about religions.

Rakwaba looked at her. "And you, young woman from America. In what do you believe?"

Carol Anne hesitated. She found it hard to come up with something that would express her feelings. "I...I believe...in the brotherhood of man," she stammered.

"Those are easy words," Rakwaba chided.

"But that's why I came here," Carol Anne said. "I wanted to *do* something."

"Why?" asked Rakwaba.

"Well, er...to help your people."

"How?"

"To teach them," Carol Anne said earnestly. "To help them help themselves."

Rakwaba sat thinking for a moment. "But you are a woman," he said. "Do you have a man?"

"No." Carol Anne looked surprised at the question.

"Do you have children?"

"No."

"Then how can you teach? To teach you must have experience, and a woman without children is without experience."

"That's not true," Carol Anne protested. "That's—ignorance. And ignorance is what keeps your people backward." Remembering something she had learned in school, she added: "Education is knowledge and knowledge brings progress."

Rakwaba laughed. "What is this 'backward'? What is this 'progress'?" You talk like a book. Books don't make life. Life makes life. For a woman, children make experience."

"A woman can get experience without having children," Carol Anne insisted, from her most liberated point of view.

Rakwaba flashed her a wise smile. "That experience is only of the body. Children are life experience. A woman must marry and bear children."

"But that's only *part* of life. In my country—"

"You are not in your country."

Carol Anne lowered her eyes.

"You're not in your country now," Rakwaba repeated sternly. "Our ways are not your ways. Here, time is our teacher. In Africa, to hear you must listen first."

Carol Anne looked thoroughly chastened. Rakwaba regarded her gravely. "You are young," he said, not unkindly. "Perhaps you will learn." Then he sat back, took up his bones, and with a wave of his hand indicated that they were to go.

Once out of the hut, they walked down the path in silence, throwing sticks for Sugar Ball to fetch.

"He likes you," said Jannie after a while.

"He likes me!" Carol Anne looked astonished. That had not been her impression at all.

"E!" Tsepo agreed, "His eyes say so." Pleased at her meeting with Rakwaba, he grabbed her hand and began to run. "Come on! You still haven't seen the waterfall!"

Carol Anne held back. "I can't go any more places. I'm tired."

"But you haven't seen anything yet!" Jannie grabbed her other hand and the two of them pulled her along the path.

Somehow Carol Anne found her second wind and bounded after the boys as they climbed among ledges and scrambled over rocks, watching giant African eagles that swept and soared over the craggy outcrops, and rock dassies that stared at them, whiskers wiggling. Despite jet lag and the unexpected heat of January, she thought about Rakwaba's words, feeling herself already changed in some way.

71

They arrived finally at their favorite place, where the cable slide was suspended through the sparkling waterfall and into the clear mountain pool below. Without even taking off their clothes, Jannie and Tsepo slid down into the pool.

"Tsepo! Jannie! Your clothes!" Carol Anne shouted.

Tsepo spurted a long stream from his mouth and then pointed up in the air. "*Ho likele*—the sun will dry them," he yelled, and then dove down again to where Jannie was swimming underwater.

For a while Carol Anne watched them enviously. She felt so sweaty and dusty. She took off her heavy boots and socks and rolled up her pants and stretched her toes toward the pool. The water looked so cool and inviting, but the only way down was via the cable.

Jannie climbed up beside her and smiled his lopsided, freckled smile. "There are no crocodiles," he said reassuringly. Then he slid down the cable and crash landed, splashing water all over her. Carol Anne jumped back with a screech, but at last she just grabbed the slide and in a second had erupted through the waterfall and hit the pool.

The shock of the cold water gave her goose bumps and the urge to jump up and down and scream like a kid. Laughing and chattering, she turned to splash Jannie and Tsepo. They splashed her back, delighted at finding someone new to play with. All three of them were splashing each other and giggling when Carol Anne happened to look up.

On a rock above them sat Father Alberto, watching the fun. With a sly grin Carol Anne scooped up some water and splashed him.

"Hey!" He jumped up, half tripping over her boots.

Still grinning, she splashed him again. But she didn't know that Father Alberto Assisi de Jesus was a trickster at heart too. With an equally mischievous smile he picked up her boots and started down the path toward the mission. "Teatime everyone!" he called.

"Come back here! Ouch! Hey!" Indignant, Carol Anne hobbled after him, her still tender feet unused to the rocky ground.

Jannie and Tsepo followed at a safe distance, giggling continuously until their stomachs were actually hurting. By the time they reached the mission, going at Carol Anne's pace, the hot African sun had dried all their clothes.

5

A few days later, just before dawn, Cash General took the leather pouch from his wall safe behind the flour bin and pulled it open to make sure the diamonds were still inside. They were. He nodded his satisfaction, pulled the drawstring tight, and stuffed the pouch into his pants pocket. He hadn't decided yet exactly what to do with the diamonds. All he could think of most of the time was how much he hated Steve Mawanga.

"I'll decide on my way to Maseru," he said to himself. He locked the safe, replaced the flour bin, and went out the front door. He hung a sign on the door that said GONE TO TOWN, and walked around to the yard where the truck was parked. He had his head down, still thinking, and it wasn't until he was right beside the truck that he saw the Spokeman. He was leaning against the door, flicking his cigarette ashes into the front seat.

Cash General's first impulse was to grab the Spokeman and bang his head against the truck, but instead he forced himself to back up against the side wall of the store, clenching his fists in his pockets to control himself. "What do you want now?" he asked.

The Spokeman smiled and lifted his spoke. "Going to town?" he asked.

Cash General always felt strong and brave in the morning. Suddenly he decided he'd had enough of Steve Mawanga and his thievery. With a look of contempt at the Spokeman he shoved him aside, spoke and all, climbed into the old battered truck and started the motor. But the Spokeman, recovering himself, thrust his spoke through the open front window and tickled Cash under the shin. "You won't forget to sell the 'cattle' will you?" he hissed softly.

The metal spoke felt cold against his skin. Cash gritted his teeth and shifted gears. "I might not even *get* to town," he growled.

"Why not?" The Spokeman looked at him suspiciously.

"Because you're leaning on the truck!" Cash shouted. He stomped the accelerator and the truck lurched forward, spewing dust and stones.

The Spokeman was thrown backward and lost his spoke in the dust. "*Moleko tooe!*" he cursed, shaking his fist at the truck, but it was already chugging up the road.

Later that morning, seated at his desk in the study, Father Alberto cast a brief glance out the window and noticed Cash's sign. Good, he thought. Perhaps they'd get the tractor tire today.

Sister Theresa was stamping her foot and sounding off at him again. "I'll have none of her fancy newfangled ideas here," she shrilled. "The very thought of it—*birth control*!

Father Alberto remained silent, looking at the folder on his desk. Sister Theresa clasped her hands prayerfully and paced the floor. "May the Lord forgive her," she murmured, "—they probably won't even know what she's talking about."

Father Alberto sighed. "Everyone is entitled to his or her own opinion, Sister. Carol Anne isn't a Catholic and she's trying to help. She'll learn." He wished she would leave so he could get to work.

Sister Theresa rapped on his desk with her ruler. "Father Alberto, you're a Catholic priest. Do you know what you're saying?"

Father Alberto nodded seriously. "Yes, Sister, Genesis, Chapter Three." Then he grinned at her, according to his resolve never to stay angry, and tried to get her to relax. "Everything will be all right, Sister. You'll see." He opened his folder of homework papers and began to work on the top one.

Taking the hint, Sister Theresa left for her class. He's always so sure that he's right and that everyone else is wrong, she thought bitterly, and he doesn't even agree with the Pope. She resolved to spend at least an hour that day praying for all their immortal souls.

Outside on the porch, Carol Anne was preparing for her first lecture. Thomas Luke, a middle-aged man from the village who knew English and who sometimes assisted at the mission, had agreed to act as interpreter. Sitting and standing in front of them in the courtyard were a group of women of varying ages, some babies, and a few old men—about thirty people in all. Everyone was gossiping happily and very much interested in what was going on. As it was market day, there were baskets of woven mats and produce that people sometimes sold to Cash or traded for other things they wanted.

Carol Anne had set up a table with appropriate leaflets and had tacked up a number of pop-art posters on the porch rails. The posters dealt in various ways with overpopulation and family planning. Carol Anne felt nervous, but she smiled, cleared her throat, and rapped on the table for attention. "Ladies of Nohateng—and gentlemen," she said. "This morning I would like to talk to you about overpopulation and family planning." She turned expectantly to Thomas Luke, but instead of merely repeating her words in Sotho, he leaned toward her across the table, a blank look on his face.

"What is that?" he asked politely. He had absolutely no idea what she meant.

Carol Anne whispered a hurried explanation while the assembled audience sat patiently, looking resigned. As her words became clear to him, Thomas Luke's eyes widened and with a terrified glance at the assembled women, he jumped up, shaking his head, and backed away. "No... it's not possible," he said hastily. "That's women's talk. I... I can't say it."

Carol Anne caught his arm. "But you must, or else how can I—" She pulled him back to the table. "All right, I'll go ahead with the pictures, and all you have to do is translate, OK?"

Thomas Luke nodded doubtfully. Carol Anne pointed to one of the posters. It showed a large red convertible filled to overflowing with an American family of thirteen. The family appeared strained but healthy. "Now this," she said clearly, "is overpopulation. The car is crowded—too full—too many children."

There was dead silence from everyone. She turned to Thomas Luke. "Translate," she urged, "translate."

"But the car is big," Thomas Luke said, puzzled.

Carol Anne was starting to get hot. She brushed the hair out of her eyes. "It's the children we're talking about, not the car," she said. "Now translate, please."

Thomas Luke turned to the audience. "The car has many children," he said. "*Koloi e kholo e nale bana ba bangata*."

Satisfied, Carol Anne pointed to another poster, which showed a smaller car with parents and two children. "Now here is a smaller family with a smaller car. It cost less and everyone's happier." She turned to Thomas Luke.

He looked at her, incredulous. "Why is the man with the smaller car happier?" he asked.

Carol Anne was losing her patience. "Just translate, Thomas," she said, rather rudely.

Thomas Luke shrugged and turned to the audience. "*Monna oa koloi e 'nyane oa iketla*," he said.

An old man in the audience looked at his wife, shaking his head at the strange logic. "The big car's much nicer," he said aloud in Sotho.

"I know, I know," Thomas Luke assured him also in Sotho. "But she is crazy in her head." Everyone else murmured their agreement. Certainly she must be crazy in the head.

Carol Anne thought their nods meant they understood. "Right!" she said enthusiastically. "Now that's basically the problem. Too many children—overpopulation!" She was delighted to have made her point. Reaching into a carton on the table, she brought out a round plastic pill dispenser. "Now these pills," she said earnestly, "are the answer to overpopulation."

Thomas Luke looked at the dispenser and shook his head. "I don't understand," he said.

Some people in the audience, anxious to see what was being offered, came closer to the porch while Carol Anne was trying to explain what she had just said. As before, when he finally understood her, Thomas Luke backed away, embarrassed and confused. To give her audience something to do in the meantime, Carol Anne began to hand out boxes of pills, leaning out over the porch rails. "Here—here," she said, as several hands reached. "The instructions are on the back. I'll explain—here—here...."

While the audience passed around the samples, Thomas Luke and Carol Anne continued their argument. "*Tsoarelo—montsoe ana* ..." he grumbled. "Such words are not for a man to speak."

"Why not?" she asked.

Several people in the audience called out to Thomas Luke, wondering about the delay, but soon everyone's attention was drawn to an old man, who had a pill in his hand and was carefully crushing it.

Carol Anne watched him in disbelief. The old man carefully stuck a fingerful of the powdered pill into a nostril, trying it out for snuff. When he didn't sneeze, he tried another. When this still didn't make him sneeze, he looked at the pill container and shrugged. Then he took a pinch of snuff from the horn he wore around his neck and sneezed—loudly. With a satisfied smile, he tossed the pill dispenser to the ground and sneezed again. Everyone laughed and began talking at once. Some of the small children began popping out the pills one by one and burying them in the dirt. Carol Anne banged desperately on the table, trying to regain their attention. "Hey, everyone be quiet!" she yelled. "I haven't finished!"

Suddenly across the yard the school bell rang for morning recess. All the school children tumbled out into the yard and hurried over to see what was going on. Over all this excitement came the honk honk honk of Cash General's truck in the distance. A few minutes later it pulled into the yard with a loud squealing of brakes and enveloped them all in a huge cloud of dust. Despite this, everyone converged on the truck and Carol Anne was left standing alone at her table.

She burst into tears, but almost immediately a comforting arm went around her shoulders. Sobbing, she buried her head in Father Alberto's chest. "Now don't cry. Come on," he said. "It was good for you."

Carol Anne tried to swallow her tears.

"Did you bother to ask whether Africans had any form of birth control of their own before you imposed your ways?" Father Alberto asked gently.

Carol Anne shook her head. "Have they?" she asked.

Father Alberto smiled. "Of course," he said, laughing. "It's self-control!"

It was Carol Anne's turn to look shocked.

Just then the truck horn began hooting continuously, and Father Alberto, still laughing, looked up and saw Cash General waving at him. Carol Anne began to collect her posters and leaflets. Feeling sorry but unable to help her further, he left her and went to the truck. Cash was just climbing out. "Did you get the tire?" Father Alberto asked.

Cash nodded and pointed to the back of the

truck. Father Alberto went around to take a look. "It's big!" yelled Tsepo, who had climbed up to see.

"It's ginormous!" Jannie shouted, jumping up and down to catch a glimpse of it.

The boys watched Father Alberto as he thumped the new tire and got ready to roll it out. "You promised us the old one," Jannie reminded him. "Didn't he, Tsepo?"

"Yes, you promised," Tsepo said. "Please?"

"I'll give you the old, but only if you help me change them," said Father Alberto.

"We will, we will!" Jannie and Tsepo began hopping up and down, shaking the truck.

"Get off!" Cash screamed. "You're bouncing the groceries! Get off or I'll throw you off!"

Later that afternoon, when school had let out, Jannie and Tsepo helped Father Alberto roll the tire into the tractor shed. They jacked up the huge tractor, using a special pulley, and changed the tire. It was almost suppertime when they finished. Tsepo went home. Father Alberto started the generator, and Jannie ran into the mission kitchen. He was delighted. "We've got our tire!" he shouted excitedly. "We've got our tire!"

Carol Anne, who was setting the table, just smiled. She was feeling a little subdued after her ordeal.

"Let's see your hands," said Sister Theresa.

Giggling, Jannie held them up in front of her face. They were covered with dirt and grease from the tractor.

"Ugh!" said Sister Theresa, backing away. "Go and be washing them, and don't forget to scrub your nails."

Jannie ran across the hallway to the bathroom and scrubbed his hands as clean as he could get them. Then he climbed up on the basin so that he could look out the high bathroom window at the tire, which was leaning against the shed wall bathed in the soft red light of the setting sun. A big grin spread over his face. He couldn't wait to play with it tomorrow.

The next day, which was Saturday and no school, Jannie and Tsepo were up early. With Sugar Ball barking at their heels, they started off rolling the tire in the courtyard in front of the mission. But by accident they rolled it into some girls on their way to Sister Theresa's sewing class. The girls scattered, giggling and dropping clothes all over the yard. Then Sister Theresa yelled at them to get the tire out of the yard, so they took it out on the road in front of the store.

Inside the store, Cash and Mama Joy were putting away the groceries he had brought from Maseru. Mama Joy came out of the backroom with six paper bags of beans in her arms. "Where do you want these?" she asked.

Cash, who had his nose in the register and was figuring out numbers, pointed vaguely to the side wall of shelves and went back to his work. Mama Joy gave him a look, pushed the ladder to the side wall with her foot, and climbed up. Just as she got the second bag on the shelf, there was a terrific BANG! on the wall. The shelf collapsed and so did Mama Joy, who went down in a spray of rice, meal, and beans. "OOOOOOO!" she shouted. "The wall hit me!"

Cash looked up in amazement. Jannie and Tsepo came running in the front door.

"Sorry," said Jannie.

"The tire," said Tsepo.

Mama Joy looked up at them from her very undignified place on the floor, surrounded by burst bags of rice and with her dress hiked up over her fat legs. "You!" she shrilled. "Wait till I get you! You and your tire!"

Jannie and Tsepo took one look at each other and dashed out the door. They decided after a whispered conference outside to play with the tire a little further away, where they could do less damage.

Carol Anne helped Sister Theresa at the sewing class. Then finding herself with nothing to do, she decided to go for a walk. The air was warm and sultry, and by the time she had crossed the road she was already sweating. She trudged up the mountain path, still depressed from her fiasco of the day before and angry that Father Alberto had allowed her to make such a fool of herself. Probably he thought it would be a good lesson for me, she said to herself, but there ought to be other ways to learn lessons. She continued to climb despite the heat and presently found herself below

Rakwaba's hut. Perhaps he would tell her more about the people of Nohateng.

She climbed up the path and after knocking as hard as she dared on the wall of the hut, ducked through the doorway and went inside. Rakwaba looked up when she came in, but didn't seem at all surprised to see her. He looked away while she settled herself, and for a long while he seemed to ignore her presence. Carol Anne accepted the silence with patience.

"What do you want?" he asked eventually.

Carol Anne was prepared. "I would like to learn more of the ways of your people," she said.

There was another long silence. "*Mokhoa o mong—tsela di fapane,*" he said. "All ways are the same. Only the paths are different." He looked at her curiously for a moment. "Why are you not in America?" he asked.

"I told you," Carol Anne said. "I came here to help."

"Are there not people in America who need help?" he asked pointedly.

"Yes," Carol Anne whispered and looked at her feet.

"Why do you wear men's shoes?" Rakwaba asked suddenly.

Carol Anne looked up again, surprised. "So my feet won't hurt," she said.

Rakwaba smiled at her. "I like your men's shoes," he said. "This is wise." He shook his polished bones and prepared to throw them.

Carol Anne smiled back, pleased that at least

there was a thread of friendship between them, but Rakwaba's smile faded when he looked down at the bones. "There are clouds that speak of danger and winds that cry of sorrow," he said, his voice anxious and strained. "There will be darkness that speaks of death and light and speaks of life." He looked up at Carol Anne, a terrified expression on his face. "You must go," he said sharply. "The winds are coming."

Frightened, Carol Anne jumped up and ran outside. "My God, he was right," she whispered. Above her the sky was dark grey and a howling wind tore at the dusty path and sent pebbles rolling. She hurried as fast as she could down to the mission.

Below her, in the village, people were running in every direction, gathering up blankets and grass mats that had been left out to dry and covering pots on outside fires. As she ran past the kraal, Mohale was securing the gate to contain some frightened goats.

Out of breath, Carol Anne ran across the road and into the dusty courtyard. Father Alberto was standing on the porch watching the storm clouds and between them the shafts of light that cast dramatic patterns on the mountains. "Have you seen Jannie?" he asked her as she ran up on the porch.

"No," she said. She looked winded and dusty. He wondered where she had been, but she didn't say anything to him at all.

They walked down the hall to the kitchen,

where Sister Theresa was making tea. "Where's Jannie?" Father Alberto asked her.

Sister Theresa looked up. "Oh, he's with Tsepo somewhere," she said, "and..."

A huge clap of thunder drowned out her words, and without finishing her sentence, she left the teapot boiling, and calling for Carol Anne to come help her, she ran to shut all the windows in the house.

Jannie and Tsepo were rolling the tire uphill along the stream. Tsepo looked up at the darkening sky. "It's going to rain," he said.

Jannie nodded. Just then there was a long low rumbling and a clap of thunder. Shivering, Sugar Ball edged closer to the boys. Tsepo looked around. "Where should we go?" he asked. They had climbed far up the hillside, where the path ran parallel to the cliffs near the mountain-that-falls-into-the-sky. There was no shelter in sight.

Jannie looked at the tire. It seemed big enough. "Let's just get inside here," he said. So they climbed in, arranged their arms and legs, including the four of Sugar Ball's, so that everyone overlapped comfortably, and awaited the downpour.

6

Teatime was fairly silent during the storm.
Afterward Carol Anne went to Father Alberto's
study to talk, but he wasn't there. She decided to
wait and took the opportunity to get a good look
at everything in the room. There wasn't much: a
bookcase full of books, a crucifix, some test
papers in a folder, and a frame with two photos.
Carol Anne leaned across the desk and looked at
the photos. On the left was a picture of Jannie,
taken at his ninth birthday party. His mouth was
covered with chocolate cake and he was grinning
into the camera. Carol Anne smiled at him. The
other photo, a Polaroid of the group at the
airstrip, was the one Cash had taken the day she
had arrived. She and Father Alberto were looking

at each other. Carol Anne stared at it a while and then put the frame back on the desk, just when Father Alberto came through the door.

He was slightly taken aback at the sight of her. "Where did you go before?" he asked.

Carol Anne hesitated. "I went to see Rakwaba," she said.

He turned to her and leaned against the sill. "Why?"

"I thought I could learn something," she said.

Father Alberto shrugged. "Sister Theresa won't like that idea."

"I'm not Sister Theresa."

That much was becoming very clear to him. Father Alberto didn't know what else to say. They looked at each other for a moment, as they had in the photo, and then he walked around behind the desk and sat down, as if to put a physical barrier between them.

Carol Anne leaned forward across the desk. "Father?"

He looked up.

"Why did you become a priest?"

His eyes darkened, as if at some memory, and she was instantly sorry that she had been so direct. But then he recovered. "That's a long, long story," he said. He smiled at her a little sadly, then tilted his chair back against the wall. "What brought you to Africa?" he asked.

Carol Anne looked away. "I don't even know any more," she admitted. "And that's a long story too."

Rakwaba sat hunched beside the fire, throwing the bones over and over. He had been doing that ever since Carol Anne had left, all during the storm. Something was wrong, very wrong, and he was frightened. He swept them up and threw them one more time. They came out the same. "The bones do not lie," he said. Jumping up, he pulled on an old jacket and hurried out of the hut. He took the path toward the mission at a pace amazing for a man his age. It was still raining lightly.

The first door he reached was the back door of Cash General's store. He knocked and then shifted impatiently from foot to foot, clenching his hand over the bones in his pocket. After a while Cash General opened the door. His mouth fell open when he saw Rakwaba. "The children—where are they?" Rakwaba asked. "*Bana ba o kae*?"

Cash just stared. "They're not here," he said. "But *uena a batlang mona*—what are you doing here?"

Rakwaba didn't answer, but started around the store on his way to the mission, leaving Cash in the doorway, looking disturbed.

Rakwaba ran across the road and onto the porch, found the doorbell, and pulled it hard. While he waited for someone to answer, he looked around. It appeared to him that nothing had changed in the fifteen years since he had been there.

Sister Theresa opened the door. She stared at

him, unable to really believe her eyes, and slammed the door in his face. Then she leaned against it on the inside, shaking with shock and anger, while Rakwaba yanked at the doorbell again and again. "What do you want?" she shouted finally.

"Jannie *le* Tsepo," he shouted back.

Sister Theresa pushed aside the curtain. "Why do you want the children?"

"*Ba kotsing*—they're in danger—*bana ba kotsing!*" he screamed, banging on the door.

But Sister Theresa wouldn't listen. "I don't understand a word you're saying," she said angrily. "Go away!" She yanked the curtain shut and ran to find Father Alberto, who was out in back working on the tractor.

The storm ended as abruptly as it had begun. Jannie poked his head out of the tire. Overhead, behind small shreds of grey cloud, the sky was clear blue. "It's stopping," he said.

Tsepo pushed out Sugar Ball and then disentangling his legs from Jannie's, climbed out. Jannie followed. Despite the protection the tire gave, their pants had gotten wet on the bottom. Jannie looked inside the tire. About an inch of water had collected in it. "It's full of water," he said.

Tsepo nodded, tugging at the tire. "We'll have to spill it out." With some difficulty, they rolled the heavy tire up and over and some of the water came out. Then they repeated the procedure, groaning with the effort, and got the rest. Tsepo looked inside. "It's all out now."

"Good," Jannie said, wiping the sweat from his forehead. "Then we can go."

They pushed the tire into position on the path and Tsepo climbed in. "Ready?" Jannie asked.

Tsepo poked his head out, grinning. "Ready," he said, and then ducked back in. Jannie began rolling the tire. It sped downward, guided by the well-worn mountain path, which formed a perfect groove for it.

"Fast—faster!" Tsepo yelled. "This is fun!" But the path led along an incline. The tire slowed and gradually came to a stop. Breathless and totally dizzy, Tsepo stumbled out. He fell flat on his back. "Ooooo—the mountains are moving!" he said.

"Silly—the mountains aren't really moving—you're just dizzy," Jannie said.

"What's that?" asked Tsepo, getting up and staggering around.

"It's when your head goes around in your head. Come on. It's my turn now," Jannie said impatiently.

But Tsepo wasn't listening. He had come to a dizzy stop at the top of the rise and remained looking down at the meandering path below, where two men were walking. They wore city clothes that were soaking wet and were obviously not in the best of moods. Something about them seemed familiar. Suddenly Tsepo remembered. Putting a finger to his lips, he motioned to Jannie, who came up beside him on the rise. "What is it?" he asked.

"Shh—look down there," Tsepo whispered.

"Who're they?" asked Jannie. "I've never seen them before."

"They're Mohale's friends," Tsepo said. "The ones that beat up Cash General."

Jannie's eyes widened. "How do you know?" he asked.

"I saw them at the kraal the night I brought the goats down late," Tsepo said.

Jannie stared angrily at the two men. "We ought to beat them up," he said.

Suddenly a mischievous expression appeared on Tsepo's face. "C'mon," he said, pulling at Jannie's arm. "We'll get them with the tire."

Jannie grinned an evil grin, and with smothered giggles they dashed back to the tire. Jannie climbed in. Hardly waiting for Jannie to settle himself, Tsepo pushed the tire over the rise. It rolled down, gathering speed, and he ran silently after it. Even Sugar Ball seemed to be in on the trick as he ran beside Tsepo without barking.

Yard by yard the tire gathered speed, going faster and faster toward Steve Mawanga and his Spokeman, who walked steadily downhill, unaware. But as it came closer to them, the tire made a slight whistling sound. Sensing something wrong, the Spokeman turned. The tire was almost upon them. "Mawanga!" the Spokeman screamed.

With a yell, Steve Mawanga leaped off the path

just in time. As the tire passed him, he lashed out and with a vicious kick pushed it off the path. The tire continued rolling over the hillside, wobbling unevenly and heading directly toward the mountain-that-falls-into-the-sky. Steve Mawanga gazed at it with satisfaction, cursing under his breath and pleased at Jannie's approaching fate.

Terrified, Tsepo began to run after the hurtling tire in a desperate, useless attempt to stop it. But it seemed like the faster he ran, the further away the tire rolled. He burst into tears. "Help!" he screamed, turning to Mawanga. "Stop it! Please help—please!" But the two men made no move and so he ran on, screaming, until his foot hit a stone. He sprawled on the slope, sobbing.

Inside the tire Jannie knew it was out of control, but he didn't know where he was going. He rocked back and forth, desperately trying to overturn it. "Help!" he screamed. "Tsepo—help!" He tried to stick out his hand, but pulled it back in, gasping in pain, when it was instantly mauled by the whirling rocks. Terrified, he pulled himself tighter into the tire, unaware that the gaping cliffs were ahead of him.

The truck screeched to a dusty stop on the road beside the river just as the tire with Jannie pinned inside hurtled over the jagged edge of the cliff. While they watched in helpless terror, the tire bounced and twisted over the rocks. It crashed finally into the ravine and then came to a stop wedged between two huge boulders in the middle of the river.

Sister Theresa looked at the little limp hand, scraped and bloody, that dangled pathetically out of one side of the tire. Turning her face away, she crossed herself and fell to her knees, sobbing hysterically.

"Take care of her," Father Alberto ordered Carol Anne. Then grabbing a rope from the back of the truck, he and Cash and Rakwaba lowered themselves down through a fault in the rock. Motioning to Cash and Rakwaba to remain at the edge of the river, Father Alberto waded to within a few yards of the trapped tire. The water between him and Jannie was a deep raging torrent. He stepped from rock to rock, balancing, trying to make his way closer, and finally plunged in. He was instantly swept downriver and pounded against the rock where the tire was. He grabbed it, slipped, then grasped the slippery rock again and pulled himself up. Quickly he tied one end of the rope to himself, leaving a long end, and then carefully extricating Jannie's smashed, limp body, he roped the child to his chest.

"Ready!" he screamed to Cash over the noise of the water.

Cash turned to Rakwaba. "Grab here and pull when he lets go." Rakwaba nodded. "Support his head!" Cash yelled.

"OK—now!"

Releasing himself backward into the river,

Father Alberto was swept in a violent arc by the rope as they pulled him across, against the current, over the sharp rocks of the riverbed, until he bumped against the bank. Rakwaba and Cash hauled in the rope and lifted him out.

As they untied Jannie and laid him on the ground, Tsepo came running along the road. Gasping for breath, he slid to his knees over the rocks, staring at the still form of his friend. Jannie's limp hand lay at a broken, awkward angle, his pale face absolutely still, his eyes shut. "Jannie," Tsepo whispered. He looked up at Father Alberto, who was kneeling beside him. "Is he dead?"

"I don't know." Father Alberto felt for Jannie's pulse but couldn't find it. Then lowering his head to Jannie's chest, he tried to listen for his heart. "I don't know," he said again, feeling helpless and confused.

From behind him Rakwaba moved in, motioning Father Alberto to stand aside. The old man knelt beside Jannie and with expert fingers began to examine him from head to toe. Gently his fingers eased over the obviously cracked ribcage, then carefully onto the area over the spleen and kidneys. Jannie gave an unconscious twitch. Rakwaba lowered his ear to the boy's chest, concentrating, then pressed the kidney area again.

Then he got to his feet and turned to Father Alberto. For the first time the two men faced each other, and the sympathy between them was immediate. Speaking softly, Rakwaba shook his head. "*Ho ho ntho e nka e etsang,*" he said. "There is nothing I can do, for *hobane o se a le mekhatheng a lefu*, he lies in the shadow of the great darkness."

Father Alberto pressed his lips together. He wanted to scream.

Rakwaba looked at him and then said hesitantly. "Perhaps the medicine of the white doctors can help him, but I don't know."

Father Alberto looked into Rakwaba's eyes that were dark with pity. "*Ke ea utloa,*" he said. "I understand."

Cash was already running to the truck. "Quickly," he called over his shoulder. "We'll take him to the hospital in Maseru."

"You have little time," Rakwaba said, as he bent down to help Father Alberto pick Jannie up.

"I know," said Father Alberto, struggling to control himself. "I'll drive fast."

7

Sister Theresa sat stiff as a statue on the hard wooden bench of the hospital waiting room. Her eyes were closed and her fingers moved across the beads of the rosary like some animal running for its life. She had been praying for hours, ever since she had seen the tire come over the cliff. She had tried to stop several times, but as soon as her mind wandered she saw the tire again and began to sob. At least the prayers controlled her, gave her something to do. "Hail Mary, full of grace," she said again, moving her lips slightly.

Beside her Carol Anne stared at the floor. The praying next to her, which she had minded at first, had become a familiar rhythm, like continuous music heard only at intervals, something one lived with and for the most part ignored. She shifted uncomfortably on the bench, recrossed her legs, and folded her arms across her chest, feeling chilly and damp and ill at ease in her dirty, bloodstained clothing. She recounted over and over their terrifying drive to the hospital in Maseru.

On the way she and Sister Theresa had held Jannie spread across their laps in the cab of the truck, and he had felt to her like a heavy, broken marionette. A while after they started it got dark and twice they had to go cautiously through flooded sections, as though fording a river. Father Alberto had driven wildly and without caution, like a crazy person. After one turn she had been suddenly terribly frightened that he might lose control. But he had not, although they drove over some of the steepest and most treacherous roads she had ever seen, not at all like the American superhighways she was used to. Carol Anne realized that she didn't really know these people very well. They had given her only conflicting information about Jannie, and when all the papers had to be signed in the emergency room there had been some confusion.

The doctor had said they'd have to wait for the X-rays, but they'd already been waiting an hour. Carol Anne looked up at the clock on the wall, which said 11, and then at Father Alberto, who stood with his back to them staring out the window. She noticed that his clothes were still wet. She couldn't tell whether he was praying or not, or she might have walked over to talk with him.

Father Alberto was looking at his truck in the small parking lot just outside the waiting room. It had started to smoke the last few miles before they reached the hospital, and he had panicked briefly thinking they wouldn't make it, giving Sister Theresa and Carol Anne orders about what to do while he ran for help. But despite his lack of faith the truck had made it. After Jannie had been put onto a stretcher and wheeled into the emergency room, he had gone back outside and raised the hood to look at the strained engine, but it had boiled up in his face and he hadn't been able to see what was wrong. There was a dark greasy stain on the floodlit pavement of the parking lot.

The sound of a door opening down the hall broke in on Sister Theresa's praying and she was immediately silent. All three of them looked up expectantly as footsteps headed in their direction. The tall doctor came in, pulling a green mask away from his face. He appeared distressed, for he was young and it was still hard for him to tell people things. He sighed and then began: "His ribs are broken. So are both his arms. But that's minor. It's his renal area that's seriously affected."

"Renal?" asked Father Alberto. "I don't—"

"His kidneys," the doctor said hastily. "He'll have to be operated on within forty-eight hours."

"Why forty-eight hours?" asked Father Alberto. "Can't you operate now?"

The doctor shook his head. "The nearest hospital capable of this operation is in Johannesburg. If I operate here, he would . . . die."

He would die. Father Alberto looked out the

window at the dripping truck. Behind him Sister Theresa was sobbing quietly. "It's over a hundred miles to Johannesburg," he said. "I can't make it. Can you take him?"

"We'll supply an ambulance," the doctor said. "I'll call right now." He disappeared down the hall again.

Ten minutes passed. Carol Anne stared at the clock the whole time. Then far down the hall they heard a phone ring. Presently the doctor returned. He came into the room more slowly this time, his expression even more strained, and sat down beside Sister Theresa on the bench. He cleared his throat and then said very quickly: "The senior renal surgeon is away. He's been sent to the New York University Hospital for six weeks to learn new techniques."

"You mean they can't do anything in Johannesburg?" Father Alberto asked, his voice rising in panic.

"Of course," the doctor said. "They're prepared to operate, but—"

"But?"

"But they don't hold out much hope."

"Then we'll have to get him to New York." It was Carol Anne who spoke.

Everyone looked at her as if she were crazy. "What are you talking about?" Father Alberto burst out angrily. "How can we get him to America! And in forty-eight hours!" He turned away from the group on the bench and leaned his head against the window.

"I can arrange it," Carol Anne said simply,

offering no further explanation, and then spoke calmly to the doctor. "There's a U.S. satellite tracking aircraft permanently stationed in Johannesburg," she said, suddenly assuming an air of quiet confidence. "Can you alert the Jan Smuts airport? And where is your telephone, please? I'd like to place an overseas call to Washington, D.C."

Outside on the runways of the Jan Smuts airport it was pouring rain, and in the Flight Operations room of the U.S. satellite tracking base all the lights were on even though it was only three in the afternoon.

The navigator on duty was getting himself a cup of coffee from the machine when his pilot barged in. "Drink up man, and then move it!" he yelled. "We're goin' home!"

"Home? What do you mean we're goin' home? You crazy, man?"

The pilot shook his head and then waved a cable in front of the navigator's face. "Read this, baby."

The navigator grabbed the paper. "By authority of William F. Duxley, U.S. Senator, Wyoming..." he read aloud. "What's it all about?"

"We're on a mercy flight," the pilot explained. "Some kid fell off a mountain and he's gotta have an operation right away in New York." He was already halfway out the door. "So get your ass moving," he called over his shoulder. "We're takin' the Senator's daughter too!"

"Yessir!" The navigator tossed the rest of his coffee into the drain, and grabbing his jacket, headed for the plane. "New York here we come. Yippee!"

An hour later, some newspaper reporters, the commanding officer of the base, and the deputy mayor of Johannesburg stood under a boarding canopy in the rain, watching the plane as it backed up slowly and then turning left rolled steadily along the runway approach. In the cockpit the pilot glanced at the navigator who checked the control panel and then nodded. "Operation Mercy Maseru ready for takeoff," the pilot said into the microphone. "Instructions please."

The radio came on and filled the cockpit with static. "Operation Mercy Maseru you're cleared for takeoff," crackled the voice from the control tower. "Runway zero three."

Behind them, in the empty cabin of the plane, Carol Anne buckled her seat belt in response to the flashing sign. Beside her in the aisle the stretcher with its gleaming chrome sides was wired securely to the next row of seats so that it wouldn't shift around. Under the blankets only the top of Jannie's head was visible, and she noticed with a sudden surge of feeling that his hair was still dirty and stuck together. Beneath her feet she felt the vibrating whine of the engines, then the bumpy few hundred yards on the runway, and then they were aloft, flying blind in the rain. After a while she undid the seat belt and curled up in the large white cotton uniform jacket someone at the hospital had loaned her. She looked out at the grey blur of the wing through the rain. There were twelve hours to go, and she did not plan on sleeping.

The reporters met their deadlines for the evening editions and even printed pictures of Jannie which they had relayed through video cable from Maseru. Not only in Johannesburg but elsewhere in South Africa, the chocolate cake picture of Jannie appeared in the news, along with an account of Operation Mercy Maseru.

In Pretoria *Die Transvaler* carried the story on the front page. Early in the evening a grey-haired woman in her late fifties took the paper from her letter box and walked through a dimly lit hallway to her living room. It was an old house Mevroew Pienaar lived in, neat and simply furnished, though poor. Her husband having died some years before, she lived alone.

She switched on the radio and sat down in an old armchair. The radio came on loud: "... at 5:40 P.M. today, the United States Air Force reconnaissance aircraft *Windborne* took off from Johannesburg on a one-stop mercy flight to New York..." Mevroew Pienaar turned down the volume and opened the paper in her lap. Then she stared in astonishment at the picture on the front page. The radio continued but she hardly heard it: "... the child injured yesterday afternoon in Lesotho will be operated on upon his arrival tomorrow..."

"...at approximately 6:00 A.M. New York time, twelve noon local time." In the mission study, Father Alberto turned up the volume on the same program. "The condition of the child is reported to be very serious. And now for local weather conditions..."

Father Alberto switched off the radio, a battery operated 1947 model left by the old priest. It was sitting on the desk. He leaned forward on his elbows beside it and looked at Sister Theresa, who was sitting by the window, looking out at the continuing drizzle that made the evening seem darker than it was. She had barely said a word since yesterday. After they had sent Carol Anne off with Jannie in the ambulance, she had ridden beside him totally silent, all during the three hours it had taken them to get back to Nohateng in the leaking truck. He would have liked to comfort her, as easily as he had been able to comfort Carol Anne after her lecture, but Sister Theresa was not someone you could easily put an arm around.

Nor did Father Alberto know what to do for himself. He looked at the bookcase and found nothing that might absorb him. Reading the titles across, he stopped at one that put him in mind of something. He got up from his desk and went to the bookcase, and pulled out a large maroon geography book. From its center fold he produced a letter, which he lowered onto Sister Theresa's lap, where she still tirelessly fingered the rosary. Startled, she looked at the address, which was in her own handwriting, and then looked up at him, puzzled.

"I'm sorry," he said. "Maybe we should have sent him away, but what would have become of him? Is an orphanage better than Nohateng?"

She looked again at the envelope, which had been opened. It was the letter she had written to the Archbishop in Maseru.

"I'm sorry," he said again, standing in front of her awkwardly. Then, unable to stay still, he got his poncho from the coatrack in the hall and went outside. Sister Theresa heard him blowing his nose. She guessed he was crying. It was the first time she ever felt sorry for him.

The rain had stopped but a fine mist hung like fog over the road and the kerosene lamps in the store were only barely visible. Father Alberto walked up the mountain path, avoiding the puddles and trying not to think.

Tsepo was sitting next to the pool, running his hand slowly back and forth along the cable slide. He looked up when he saw Father Alberto and then buried his face in Sugar Ball's fur. The dog sat next to him, looking just as dejected. "It's all my fault," Tsepo said, his voice muffled in the fur.

Father Alberto sat down beside him and patted Tsepo's shoulder. "No it isn't," he said.

Tsepo shook his head. "Yes it is."

"No," Father Alberto insisted gently. "You mustn't blame yourself. It was Steve Mawanga's fault, if anyone's, and Jannie's in God's hands now."

Tsepo shrugged and looked up. "I don't believe in your God," he said.

"That's not true," Father Alberto said.

Tsepo shook his head. "But I don't. I believe in *Badimo*. I'm sure of it."

"What's that?" asked Father Alberto.

"Rakwaba's God," Tsepo said.

"Oh."

"Jannie believes in your God," Tsepo offered, conciliatory.

"Yes, I suppose he does," said Father Alberto. He thought of Jannie, the still pale form on the stretcher as they wheeled it into the ambulance.

"But Father, how can your God let such a thing happen to Jannie?"

Father Alberto stared into the pool, a swirl of light and dark, struggling to explain his acceptance, his resignation to God's will. "Only God knows why it happened," he said, feeling stupid and inadequate, "so we can only hope and pray that He will save Jannie."

Tsepo didn't answer. He threw a stone into the water. They heard it splash, but it had gotten too dark to see. "You'd better come home now," Father Alberto said, rising. "Your family will worry."

They walked down the mountain in silence, picking their way among the ruts and over the stones dislodged by the rain. Father Alberto left Tsepo at his home and went down to the mission, but paused at the front door with his hand on the knob, unwilling to go in. With Jannie and Carol Anne both gone the silence was eerie and threatening. Again he wished that he could comfort Sister Theresa, but didn't know how, and then it occurred to him that he wished she could comfort him. But he wanted to talk and she could only pray. With a sigh that was almost a sob, he withdrew his hand from the doorknob, retraced his steps and went across the road to the store, where a light was burning in the back room.

Tsepo went to bed, but he couldn't sleep. He got up and crawled quietly past his sleeping parents and past the grass curtain. Outside in the moonlight the village was silent. Far up on the mountain he could see a faint glow from a small fire in front of Rakwaba's hut, and Tsepo knew the old man would be awake, throwing his polished bones. But it was not Rakwaba he wished to see. Instead he went down the path and across the road to the mission chapel, which was always left open, and let himself in the outside door.

At the front of the room one flickering candle, near its end, lit up the empty pews. Tsepo slid into a back pew and knelt on the musty, cloth covered cushion. "*Oho modimo oa babasoeu,*" he whispered. "God of the white man—and of Jannie—please save him like Father Alberto said."

Suddenly a sound came from the entrance into the mission house, and the door opened slowly. Tsepo turned. It was Sister Theresa. She went to the front, lit another candle, and then as the room brightened, she noticed the small figure in the back pew. Walking slowly and tiredly in her flapping slippers she came to the back, knelt beside him, and prayed.

On the other side of the road, in the back room of the store, Cash General and Mama Joy were playing cards. After his fourth loss in a row Cash General put down his hand and glanced across the room at Father Alberto, who had been quietly sitting in an old chair in the corner. He was asleep. "Should I wake him and send him to bed?" he asked.

"No no," said Mama Joy sadly. "Just let him be."

Carol Anne walked out of the hospital elevator beside the rolling stretcher, holding tightly to its chrome bars to steady herself and to connect herself to something. In the bright lights and sudden cold she felt as though she were walking through a nightmare. Beside her walked two silent men, the stretcher crew who had met them at the airport, and a nurse. As soon as they were all out, the elevator doors closed with a muffled whoosh. The nurse looked at Carol Anne. "You'll have to wait here," she said briskly, with a glance at Carol Anne's hand.

She nodded and let go of the stretcher, suddenly terrified that the operation was going to actually happen at last. She stood off to one side while they wheeled Jannie past her through a set of thick padded double doors into the operating room. Behind them the doors thumped shut. Immediately a red light flashed on and below it a neon sign that said DO NOT ENTER WHILE RED LIGHT IS ON. Carol Anne turned away and walked to the window, feeling terribly alone.

Outside the buildings of New York twinkled against a cold black starless February sky. With a shiver she sat down on the hard wooden bench in the waiting room, thinking at once of the one just like it in the hospital at Maseru, of Sister Theresa praying beside her and Father Alberto's back as he had stood staring out the window in his wet clothes. "Oh God," she said wearily. The clock on the wall said two. She slumped inside the overcoat, also borrowed, that she had put on over the borrowed cotton doctor's jacket, and fell into an exhausted sleep.

The hand on her shoulder was gentle but demanding. "Miss Duxley?" a voice asked, and then, "Miss Duxley, can I get you a cup of coffee?"

"Yes." Carol Anne woke up with the word on her lips, suddenly aware that someone was sitting beside her on the bench. "Yes," she said again.

The man was wearing a green suit. "Miss Duxley, I am Dr. Martens from Johannesburg," he said.

Carol Anne nodded at him. "And this is Dr. Benson, my colleague from New York."

Carol Anne noticed another green suit and nodded again. Someone put a paper cup of coffee in her hand.

"His kidneys were very badly damaged," Dr. Benson said. "We had to remove the suprarenal glands, so his body will no longer produce any of the adrenocortical hormones."

Carol Anne just looked at them. What did it mean? There was more coming, she knew.

"Until he is conscious, we'll replace them intravenously," said Dr. Martens, "and when he is able, he will have to take pills."

"For how long?" asked Carol Anne.

Dr. Martens put his hand on her shoulder. "For the rest of his life," he said quietly.

8

It took a week for Carol Anne's first letter to reach them, after her initial cable that the operation had been performed. Father Alberto came running into the study, where Sister Theresa was waiting, ripping open the envelope as he ran.

"So far," he read aloud, "the operation has been a success. But Jannie is still in a coma, which they say is not too good." He stopped to catch his breath and to wipe his face, for although it was still early in the morning he was already sweating. "I am staying in a hotel near the hospital," he continued, "which is very convenient, and my father flew up from Washington for a few hours yesterday. But New York is cold and lonely, and I miss Nohateng. I will write when there is further news. Love, Carol Anne."

Father Alberto dropped the letter on the desk and then sat down with a sigh and looked at Sister Theresa.

Her expression was one of immense relief.

A week later, Carol Anne stretched her legs and settled herself into a more comfortable position on the green molded plastic chair in the hospital canteen. It was about 11 in the morning, and beside her the steam hissed in the radiator. A pale square of winter sun illuminated the blank sheet of paper in front of her. She looked at the paper, her mind as blank as it was, but she took up the pen dutifully. Although two weeks had passed since the operation, there was nothing new to report, but she felt she had to write anyway. "Dear Father," she wrote, and then someone tapped her on the shoulder.

"Miss Duxley?"

Carol Anne turned around. It was Dr. Benson. "Will you come with me please?" he asked. His expression was grave.

Carol Anne dropped the pen. "Is there something the matter?" she asked, feeling suddenly panicky. She followed him into Jannie's room at the end of the hall. Dr. Martens and another doctor, one she hadn't seen before, were talking in whispers and referring from time to time to the chart that hung at the foot of Jannie's bed.

"What's the matter?" she asked again. Nothing about Jannie seemed to have changed. He lay, pale and unmoving in the large bed. Two intravenous bottles hung above him and fed through long pale yellow tubes into his right upper arm. Both his lower arms were encased in plaster casts. Carol Anne had grown used to seeing him this way, day after day, night after night—the same pale face and unmoving body. She could barely remember the real Jannie.

"Miss Duxley, this is Dr. Stanton." Dr. Martens was indicating the stranger beside him.

Carol Anne nodded. Obviously, something was very wrong.

"Clinically, there is nothing wrong," Dr. Martens began, "but some deterioration—"

"When did deterioration set in?" asked the new Dr. Stanton, who had a grey beard. He looked very concerned.

"It's been slow. We can't understand it. Medically, he's OK," Dr. Benson explained.

Deterioration. Carol Anne looked away from them at the intravenous bottles, which had begun to sway slightly.

"He's turning his head," said Dr. Stanton.

"That's the only movement he ever makes," said Dr. Martens.

Jannie rolled his head restlessly from side to side. "Tsepo," he whispered very faintly. "Tsepo."

"What's that he's saying?" Dr. Stanton bent over the tiny figure in the bed.

"It's the name of his friend in Lesotho," Carol Anne explained.

"A friend?"

"Another little boy. They were together at the time of the accident," she said. "They're always together. It's like he's calling him, you know?"

"Unconsciously he probably is," Dr. Stanton agreed. He looked at Jannie, and then spoke with authority to the other doctors. "If you have any hope of reversing the deterioration," he said, "I would suggest you get this Tsepo here at once."

"I'll send a cable right away," said Carol Anne.

The mail plane made a special trip to drop the cable, flying over Nohateng and dipping its wings twice to let them know. Father Alberto drove to the airstrip in a panic. So worried was he about what it might be that he was afraid to open it by himself. He drove the five miles back to the mission with the unopened plastic drop packet on the seat beside him.

Everyone was waiting anxiously in the back of the store, even Sister Theresa, who had lately given up her hostility to Cash General and had even found some comfort in talking about sewing with Mama Joy. When the bell rang as Father Alberto came in the door with the unopened packet, they all crowded around, and it was Cash General who finally opened it. But the cable was addressed to Father Alberto. Cash handed it to him.

"It's from Carol Anne," he said, ripping open the envelope.

"Just read it," said Sister Theresa impatiently.

JANNIE STILL IN COMA STOP SPECIALIST SAYS ESSENTIAL YOU BRING TSEPO TO NEW YORK SOONEST STOP LOVE CAROL ANNE.

There was dead silence for a moment. Then the

115

front door banged open, the bell jangling, and Tsepo dashed in. He had been in the tractor shed making a koloi, a wire cart, for Jannie to play with when he came home. "What is it, Father?" he asked. "What did the plane say?"

Mama Joy gave him a big hug that threatened to suffocate him entirely. "They've asked for you to go to New York," she said. "Jannie needs you to help him get better."

Sister Theresa looked at Father Alberto, who was reading the cable over and over. "You have to go with him," she said.

"I guess so," he responded. "But how can we ... I ... where are we going to get the money?"

Cash General looked at Mama Joy and then winked, slowly and deliberately. "Money's not a problem," he said.

Father Alberto stared at him, puzzled, but Mama Joy got the message right away. "No, money's no problem," she said. "No problem at all." She gave Tsepo another hug and immediately began to plan the trip. Mama Joy was a terrific organizer.

The shebeen was packed. The smoke was so thick it was impossible to see from one end of the store to the other. That is, if anyone could have seen through the people, who were wall to wall and dancing. In front of the grocery counter a sign in hastily printed large letters announced: BIG DRINKS—DOUBLE PRICE. Behind the counter stood two cashiers and a bartender, the cashiers being Father Alberto and Cash General, and the bartender Mama Joy. Father Alberto had his sleeves rolled up, and with his eyes squinted to keep out the smoke he could have passed for a desk clerk in a wild west saloon.

A laughing young man came to the counter and ordered whiskey with a beer chaser. Laughing back at him, Mama Joy filled a shot glass to the brim and gave him a full pint of beer. "Thanks," he said, delighted at her generosity.

"That'll be seven rand fifty," said Father Alberto, extending his hand.

"What!" The young man stopped laughing.

Like an accomplished collector, Father Alberto stood with his hand out until the customer reluctantly paid up. Then with a satisfied leer he dropped the money into a cash box on the counter.

"Two beers please!" The next customer was a young woman.

Mama Joy slid two quart bottles over the counter. "Five rand to the Father," she said cheerfully.

"Five rand!" cried the astonished young woman.

Cash General leaned over the counter and rolled his eyes at her. "That's right—five rand!"

Giggling, she handed over the money, and Cash General bounced back to his seat, smiling an evil grin at Father Alberto.

"Such a business!" said Father Alberto, mimicking Sister Theresa perfectly. "And to think that the Lord has forbidden it!" He shook his head.

"It's not that the Lord has forbidden it," retorted Cash General, "it's just that the Devil got to it first!"

They laughed and slapped each other on the back, unaware that behind them the back door had opened and shut quietly and that Steve Mawanga's Spokeman had come into the room.

Father Alberto noticed him first. The Spokeman was staring at the front door, and Father Alberto followed his gaze. The front door began opening slowly. Suddenly it slammed all the way open with a crash, the bell jangling wildly. Everyone in the shebeen stopped talking and turned around to look. But there was no one at the door, only the empty doorway framing a square of black night.

"Evening everybody," said a voice from outside, and then Steve Mawanga glided suddenly out of the darkness, nattily dressed in city clothes, and with a cane in his hand. He shut the door behind him.

"Evening Cash, Mama Joy," he said. "Some party you've got going." He sauntered around the room for a while and then stopped at the counter, gazing with an amused smile at Father Alberto. "Ah, I heard you were here, Father," he said. "And filling your pockets, I see." With a nod he indicated the cash box. Then he glared at Cash General. "Where's my money, Cash? The money for my cattle." He rested his free hand on the counter and began to drum on it with his fingers.

Cash looked at him with hatred but without surprise. He'd had a feeling that something like this would happen. He hadn't sold the diamonds, either. Reluctantly, he reached into his pocket for the pouch and then pushed it across the counter, resting his other hand protectively on top of the cash box. "Take your diamonds, but you can't have this," he said. "This money's for—"

Mawanga let him get no further. Angered at the sight of the unsold diamonds, he raised his cane and laid a vicious stroke across the back of Cash General's hand. Wincing in pain, Cash drew his hand to his chest and held it there, his lips pressed together to keep from crying out.

No one moved. Steve Mawanga picked up the pouch and put it into his pocket. Then he opened the cash box. "That's a lot of money you've got there, Father," he said, almost respectfully, and then glancing at the Spokeman, added: "Lock the front door, we don't want anyone stealing this. Do we?" he asked Father Alberto.

Father Alberto clenched his fists under the counter. He felt himself trembling with rage and wanting to fight this man who caused other people so much pain. But he was also afraid. He knew enough about Steve Mawanga and his activities to know he *ought* to be afraid.

"Do we, Father?" Mawanga repeated, raising his cane slightly.

Father Alberto flinched. "No," he whispered.

"Good. Now Mama, how about a drink?"

With trembling hands Mama Joy poured a whiskey for him and slid it across the counter. Steve Mawanga pulled up a chair and sitting down opposite Father Alberto reached into his pocket and brought out a wallet. "What's this, Father?" he asked.

"A wallet," Father Alberto answered quickly, needing no prompting this time.

Steve Mawanga handed it to him. "What's in the wallet?" he asked.

Father Alberto looked inside. "It's empty," he said.

"That's right," Steve Mawanga said, as though he were talking to a child. "It's empty and it needs filling. Start with the notes: tens on one side, ones on the other, and fives in the middle. And the coins I'll just take in the bag with my cattle." He sat back with a big grin and sipped his drink.

Father Alberto put the wallet on the counter. Moving slowly, he drew the cash box toward him and began emptying the coins into the bag of diamonds, directly opposite Steve Mawanga's evil, self-satisfied grin. There was something about that grin that forced him into a final reckoning. Like Cash General's reaction at dawn to the Spokeman, Father Alberto had finally had enough. Evil had to be fought, he thought. And I'm strong, he said to himself. I can beat him. Which was true. Father Alberto had a farmer's arms and a mechanic's agility because he was both.

He watched Steve Mawanga while he finished

transferring the coins, trying to decide what to do next. Before taking out the bills he hesitated, then bending over the counter, motioned to Steve Mawanga that he wished to tell him something. Mawanga rose and leaned toward him, and before he could react, Father Alberto's hands had streaked up and across his back and grabbed his fancy jacket at the neck. He pulled Mawanga forward and upward in one movement, and then smashed his face full force onto the bag of coins and stones. Unable to control himself, he smashed it again. Then, horrified at what he'd done, he let go.

Dazed, Mawanga lifted his bruised face and staggered backward, though he recovered enough to raise his cane in the air. But it never came down. Father Alberto dashed out from behind the counter and let fly a powerhouse left hook, right in Steve Mawanga's face. He smashed into the wall, his cane clattering to the floor, but he was not finished. He would certainly not be outdone by a priest. Wiping his face with his sleeve, he lifted a bottle from a table beside him and shattered it against the wall. Then he advanced toward Father Alberto, the jagged neck of the bottle in his hand.

That was enough for Cash General. Jumping in front of Father Alberto, he spoke a quiet warning to Steve Mawanga, shaking his head. "*O se ke be wa mo ama*," he said.

Ignoring him, Steve Mawanga stepped sideways, still reaching for Father Alberto. "I warned you not to touch him," Cash said again, and putting his full weight behind his good fist, he slammed it into Steve Mawanga's stomach. As though all the air had been let out of him, the gangster crumpled to the floor.

But they had forgotten to watch out for the Spokeman, who had sneaked his way through the crowd and now made a dive for Father Alberto's back. "Father, watch out!" someone yelled, and then suddenly all hell broke loose. The shebeen was in an uproar. Father Alberto, remembering old Army tactics, threw the Spokeman over his head onto a table, in a very classy move. Everyone cheered wildly. When the dazed Spokeman tried to struggle to his feet, Mama Joy hit him over the head with a bottle of brandy and the Spokeman went down for the count. Then she wiped her hands on her skirt and walked majestically to the record player. She got it going full blast. Everyone began to dance.

Meanwhile Cash was going through the unconscious Steve Mawanga's pockets. He found another wallet, this one full, and a gold watch and chain. "Thanks for the donation, Mawanga," he boomed over the noise. "You can go now." Motioning for Father Alberto to come help him, he opened the front door. Then the two of them grabbed Mawanga by his jacket and the seat of his pants and heaved him out the door into the dust.

"Hey, here's another for you," yelled Mama Joy, pointing at the Spokeman. Father Alberto and Cash General repeated the procedure, and then they slammed the door.

Father Alberto was breathing heavily but he had a big wide grin on his face. "You know what, Cash?" he gasped, in a wonderful Irish brogue. "May the Lord forgive me, but I'll be blessed if I didn't enjoy that!"

The next morning Father Alberto was in the most incredibly good mood. There was plenty of money to go and they were going. In the bargain they had got rid of Steve Mawanga, at least for a while. He emptied the proceeds of the shebeen onto his desk to show Sister Theresa. Her eyes widened as she watched first the paper money, then the coins, the gold watch and chain, and finally the uncut diamonds as they spilled out all over the desk. "All that?" she said dubiously, as usual immediately suspicious.

"Oh, and it was a wonderful donation," he assured her in his fake Irish brogue. "Everyone gave willingly—even Mawanga. You should have seen him..."

Sister Theresa's expression remained doubtful, but nothing would destroy his good mood. He looked at her narrow prim figure in the dusty white habit and decided she needed to have the dust shaken out of her. He began prowling toward her, his head lowered and his face in a wide menacing grin. "Sister, be happy!" he shouted. "We're going to America to help Jannie get well!" Startled, she backed away, but he grabbed her and lifted her up and whirled her around in the air. "Whee!" he yelled. "Wheeee!"

"Father!" she screamed, struggling and pounding on his head with her fists. "Father, put me down this minute—this minute!"

Undaunted, he held her in the air. "Why Sister," he shouted, whirling her around once more, "you're a few feet closer to heaven now!"

"Put me down!"

Across the road, Cash heard the noise but paid it no mind. He figured they were just having another argument. He and Mama Joy were in the back of the store, looking through magazines, trying to come up with something suitable for Tsepo to wear. "Here's something," said Cash finally. He gave her a picture of a small American boy in a grey flannel suit. "We'll make him a suit, just like that."

"From what?" asked Mama Joy.

Cash thought a minute, then ran to the front room. "I've got it!" he yelled, and returned with a thick grey Lesotho blanket.

"But Cash, that's a blanket," she said.

"Mama," said Cash, putting his arms around her and giving her a big squeeze, "the way you sew—*khedi*—no one will ever know the difference!"

"Ah, you," said Mama Joy, and wiggling out of his grasp, went to consult with Tsepo's mother about his size.

Several days later Tsepo stood sweating in his new suit and sneakers and slightly embarrassed by all the fuss. "They'll get so dirty," he complained, pointing to the clean white sneakers.

"Oh, you'll get used to that," Cash General said. "They'll be dirty in no time. In America, everyone wears dirty sneakers. I saw it in a magazine."

"No, they wear boots," said Tsepo. "Jannie said so, and Carol Anne does."

Mama Joy adjusted the lapels on her handiwork and then gave Tsepo a big emotional smile. "You look just like a man," she said sentimentally. Then, remembering something, she got a rand note out of the cash register and stuck it in Tsepo's breast pocket. "Here," she said, patting it down flat. "Just in case. OK?"

Tsepo looked at her and grinned. "OK!" Then, still grinning at both of them, he slipped a lollipop into his pocket on the way out of the store. He took a red one, intending to give it to Jannie, since that was his favorite flavor.

It was a blinding hot day. Heat waves shimmered above the rocks. He walked up the path, scuffing the dust onto his sneakers, feeling sweaty and uncomfortable in the heavy suit. By the time he got up the mountain he had taken off the jacket and was carrying it over his arm, taking pains to see that his ketie didn't fall out of the pocket. Cash had advised him to take it for protection.

Off and on, as he climbed, he heard the clang of something being pounded on a rock. When he arrived at Rakwaba's hut, he found that the old man had prepared a charm for him to wear around his neck. It was a tiny goat's horn strung on a leather thong. Packed down in the horn were aromatic herbs that smelled good.

Rakwaba hung the charm around Tsepo's neck. "*Eena ke metso la lefatse,*" he said. "Inside this horn are the roots of the earth from where you come. They will protect you when you are on the other side of the world."

Tsepo rubbed his fingers along the smooth polished horn. "Thank you, Rakwaba," he said softly. He was very pleased to wear it.

Rakwaba smiled at him and patted his head. "Now go," he said. "Your friend is waiting across the water. The bones tell me he is calling you."

Tsepo ran down the path, stopping once to wave goodbye again. Rakwaba watched him, feeling a pang as the boy disappeared from view. Of all the children of Nohateng, Tsepo was the only one to whom he felt the secrets of the *Badimo* should be revealed. Rakwaba intended to teach him everything before he died.

Cash General was driving them to Maseru. Tsepo sat in the middle, small and hot in his suit, clutching his tin box which he would not part with. Father Alberto sat beside him, uncomfortable also in the clerical collar and ancient black suit, neither of which he had worn in almost a decade. He was surprised they still fit, and he thought they looked awful.

Sister Theresa came up to the window. "Father," she said softly. He turned. She thought he looked wonderful in his collar and suit. There were tears in her eyes. Surprised, Father Alberto

126

reached for her hand, but she pulled away. "Just bring him back—alive and well," she said.

"We will." He smiled at her as the truck moved off along the dusty road, hoping she'd be all right. He wasn't at all sure whether she could start the generator.

The last thing Tsepo noticed as the train pulled out of Maseru was Cash General's bald head, glistening with sweat. He was the only one left on the platform, and he was still waving goodbye.

The train trip to Johannesburg took all the rest of the day. They traveled over beautiful country, through golden wheat fields, glowing in the afternoon sun, past cattle and sheep and turning windmills, and villages nestled among low green hills. Tsepo waved at everyone he saw, and some waved back. At six, their customary suppertime, they ate sandwiches from a basket that Sister Theresa had packed for them. Just as it began to get dark, they reached the outskirts of Johannesburg. Maseru had been big enough for Tsepo after a life in Nohateng, but Johannesburg was beyond his comprehension.

"This is a city, Tsepo," said Father Alberto. "*Caudeng*."

"It's bigger than Maseru," said Tsepo.

Father Alberto smiled and hugged him. "And if you think Johannesburg is big, just wait till you see New York."

Tsepo just shook his head.

From the train station they immediately took a

cab to the airport, since they didn't have too much time to make the flight. Father Alberto began to feel terribly anxious about missing the plane. They were in the airport men's room when their flight to New York was called. "Come on, hurry," he said. "They've announced the plane."

"But I haven't finished," said Tsepo.

"Well hurry anyway!"

Father Alberto's so nervous he sounds like Sister Theresa, Tsepo thought.

Their next stop was the personal baggage search booth. The search officer frisked Father Alberto, though not too carefully, out of respect for the clerical collar, and then motioned him on. Then he turned to Tsepo, who was still clutching his tin box. Ignoring the box, the officer began to frisk him. Suddenly his hand stopped at Tsepo's side jacket pocket. "What's this for?" he demanded, pulling out the ketie.

Tsepo regarded him solemnly. "*Ntate* Cash General says bad things can happen to a person in New York."

The officer burst out laughing. "Well, I doubt if it'll do you much good," he said, and then passed Tsepo through to Father Alberto.

"Hurry!" Father Alberto yelled, as if that were the only word he knew. He grabbed Tsepo's hand and they ran down the long passageway through the departures gate and came out into the grey evening. The plane, a 747 jumbo jet, loomed like a giant on the apron in front of them, The fuel trucks were departing and it was ready to go. "Hurry!" Father Alberto yelled again.

"This airplane is as big as a mountain," Tsepo panted. He held on extra tight to his tin box, while Father Alberto all but dragged him up the long stairway toward the small, high door.

It was late, almost eight, when Sister Theresa remembered about the generator. She went out to the shed, fumbling in the half dark, convinced that she'd have to call Cash or someone from the village to help her. When she struggled with the fuel can her habit hung in front of her face and obscured her view, but to her amazement the generator started after only one turn of the wheel. A delicious feeling of satisfaction settled over her soul. "Well, how's that!" she said aloud, and then, a little embarrassed to catch herself talking to no one, said "Praise the Lord," and flap-flapped in her slippers across the dirt floor of the shed and went back into the house.

The stillness there was unfamiliar and certainly trying. Sister Theresa ate and did the dishes as quickly as she could, hating the echoing clatter of the pots in the otherwise silent kitchen. She had almost grown used to having Carol Anne with her when she did the dishes. She remembered suddenly how pleased she had been when the girl had stepped up to the sink her first morning in Nohateng. "Ah, she's a good girl in many ways," Sister Theresa said to herself. "It's just that she's so dreadfully *modern*." She wondered if Father Alberto would turn modern, too, in New York.

After she finished up in the kitchen, she went

into the study and stood looking around, not at all sure what she was after but aware that it was still too early for bed. Absently, she picked up the photo frame and smiled at Jannie's chocolate cake face and the funny familiar group at the airport. Then, distracted by a scratching sound on the porch, she went out into the hall and pulled open the front door. There, head resting between front paws, sat Sugar Ball, looking at her with doleful eyes. She scooped him up, unmindful of the long streaks of dust he smeared on her habit. "Oh, you poor little dear," she crooned softly. "We're missing them too, you know." Then, with the dog still cradled in her arms, she walked slowly and thoughtfully down the echoing hall to her room.

9

At Kennedy International Airport it was 4:00 P.M. rush hour and busy enough to be Christmas if it hadn't been March. All the transatlantic flights had just arrived at once. The main arrivals hall swirled with moving people; the loudspeakers were going full blast in a nearly indistinguishable excess of instruction: "Passengers arrving on flights Panam three one seven United two one six exits zero one and three," it blared, "Swissair exit five Transworld seven oh nine..."

Tsepo was sitting rather comfortably knees to chin on the conveyor belt at Customs, waiting for their luggage to arrive. The tin box was balanced on his knees. All around him porters and passengers streamed past, collecting baggage from several flights and scrambling for places on lines. All of a sudden the man at the Customs desk switched on the conveyor belt. Taken by surprise, Tsepo scrambled off in fright as it began to move. Clutching his box, his heart pounding, he turned and watched a ton of luggage thundering down the conveyor on its way to the desk. "Ooooo," he said. "My ketie wouldn't have done much good against that!"

He stood beside Father Alberto on line, but Father was too busy gawking at everyone to pay Tsepo any mind at all. Father Alberto was thoroughly absorbed in the amazing scene before him: men and women seemed to be dressed alike, and often he couldn't tell them apart. There were many young women wearing boots and blue jeans, like Carol Anne, but he didn't see her. He wondered if she was waiting at the other end of the customs room behind the frosted glass. She was supposed to meet them.

When their turn came at Customs, Tsepo went first. "What's that?" asked the Customs official, pointing at the tin box. He was a dapper man, wearing an elegant, well-pressed uniform.

"It's my box," Tsepo said shyly. The Customs official glanced inquiringly at Father Alberto.

"Oh, that's nothing," said the priest, rather vaguely. He was looking at the shapes behind the frosted glass.

"Well, let's have a look at it anyway," said the Customs official, with a slight frown. Reluctantly, Tsepo handed him the box. The Customs official opened it and then jumped back. "Aaaaggghh!" he yelled, dropping the box on the counter. Everyone nearby turned around to look. From the open overturned box marched a slow parade of half dead lizards, scorpions, toads and beetles—the usual contents of Tsepo's box. The Customs official glared at Father Alberto. "Nothing in there, eh?" he muttered. Then he said icily: "We'll have to confiscate that, but kindly get them back in the box first."

Tsepo didn't mind losing the *mampharoane* because he knew he could always get more, but he did mind losing the box because they had stopped ordering that kind of tea at the mission and he knew he couldn't get another. He started to make a fuss, but Father Alberto hauled him by the hand, promising at least two new boxes, if he would only come along.

Next they got on another long line to wait for their passports to be stamped and returned. After a few minutes, Tsepo had to pee.

"Must you?" asked Father Alberto.

Tsepo nodded seriously and then jumped around to illustrate the urgency of his need. Father Alberto looked at the line. There were now about twenty people in back of them and he didn't want to lose his place. "Can you go yourself?" he asked. "It's right over there, see?"

Though Tsepo didn't feel too confident, he started across the room, working his way slowly through the crowd toward the bathrooms, which were on the other side of a long hall. When he arrived he found there were two doors, side by side. In the confusion he forgot his English words, and chose the door marked LADIES. Just as he reached up for the knob, the door was pushed open from the inside. Confronting him was a large woman, whose wide body, topped with an imposing Afro hair style, quite filled the doorway. The wide woman was leading a group of schoolgirls, all wearing tags and all about Tsepo's size. She immediately seized his hand. "What are you doin' comin' into the ladies' room?" she demanded. "What's the matter with you? You know better than that!"

Tsepo hadn't understood a word because she spoke so fast. He gaped at her, but she didn't even bother to look down at him again. The hallway traffic was very confusing, Mrs. Jackson was afraid of losing her girls, and she was late. Although Tsepo struggled some to get loose from her, she kept a firm grip on his hand, paying his struggle no attention at all, as if she somehow expected him to squirm.

She led him swiftly down the hall at the head of the line of giggling girls. At the end of the hall double doors opened out onto a long platform where several buses were parked. One, marked P.S. 186 Manhattan SPECIAL, had its doors open and its motor running. Tsepo found himself dragged up the high steps and shoved firmly into a seat by a window. One of the girls sat down beside him, on the aisle.

The bus was already full of children. As soon as

they boarded, the front doors slammed together and the bus pulled out into traffic. Within minutes, they had joined the flow of cars and trucks on a highway leading into the city. It was the end of a grey March day. Dirty slush was piled at the edges of the roads, the remains of a late winter snow. Tsepo huddled in the seat, mute and confused, cold even in his warm suit. The wide woman was sitting a few seats ahead. He knew he should try to speak to her, but she loomed so large that his English refused to come to mind.

After a while the girl next to him began to stare. He could feel her eyes even though his head was turned away. "Hey," she said, poking him. "I ain't never seen you before. What's your name?"

He turned to her. She was pretty and her rows of braids reminded him of Miriam at home. "Tsepo," he mumbled. "My name is Tsepo."

"Tsepo?" She wrinkled her nose, looking him over carefully. "Where'd you get that funny suit?"

"Mama Joy made it." Embarrassed, Tsepo turned away from her direct gaze and looked out the window again. The little girl leaned across the aisle and whispered something to another girl, who was sitting opposite her.

"Let me see," the second girl said, leaning forward.

"See what?" asked the boy next to her.

"A weird kid," she said. She stood up to get a good look at Tsepo. "Hey, he's not in our class," she added loudly.

At this all the children in the surrounding seats

began jumping up to look at Tsepo and several got out of their seats to crowd around. "Whose class are you in?" someone demanded. "Who's your teacher?"

"Sister Theresa," Tsepo whispered.

"Who?"

"Hey man, he ain't even from our school," said one boy. "I know every person in our school and he ain't in it."

"I'm gonna tell Mrs. Jackson," said a girl.

By this time all the children in the bus were craning their necks and climbing over seat backs to see, and having a good laugh at Tsepo's grey Lesotho blanket suit.

Mrs. Jackson loomed in the aisle. "Sit down everyone, what's going on here?"

"He ain't from our school," the boy who knew everyone reiterated.

"Not from our school?" the teacher echoed. She peered down. "Where you from son? What school?"

"Nohateng," Tsepo said, after a moment's hesitation. Mrs. Jackson was even bigger than Mama Joy.

"Where? Speak up, son. Don't be afraid."

"Nohateng," he said, louder.

The teacher looked confused. "Where's that?" she asked.

"Lesotho," Tsepo said, as clearly as he could. She *had* to understand that.

But Mrs. Jackson shook her head. "I'm not familiar with it," she said crossly. "Is that in the Bronx?"

Tsepo shook his head.

"Out in Queens?"

Tsepo just stared at her. The teacher gave him a last doubtful look and then went forward to speak to the driver. "Sam, listen, you'd better stop at the Precinct first before we get back to school. We picked up one that isn't ours."

The bus continued speeding toward the city, and one by one the children went back to their seats, though they turned to stare at him from time to time. Tsepo felt desolate and on the verge of tears, and it took all his concentration to keep from wetting his pants, for by this time he was desperate to pee.

After an interminable length of time the bus stopped on a city street in front of a grey stone building with green lights. The doors slid open and Mrs. Jackson stood up. "Come on, Sonny," she said, holding out her hand.

Tsepo climbed over the girl next to him into the aisle, but then remembering the teacher's iron grip on him in the airport terminal, thought better of taking her hand. Instead he pushed past her wide skirt and ran down the steps.

"Hey, come back here! Stop!" Mrs. Jackson maneuvered herself out the door but by the time she got down on the street Tsepo had disappeared around the corner. "Oh oh, let me get someone to catch him, Sam," she said. "I'll be right back." Then she hurried up the steps to the police station.

Father Alberto returned from the men's room and went straight to the information desk, where

Carol Anne was waiting with the luggage. "No, we haven't seen him, Father," said the hostess. "We've announced it three times, and there's been no response. I suggest you contact Security. They're right down the hall."

"Thank you," Carol Anne said.

Father Alberto had turned pale grey. The swirling people, the lights and sounds, made him think he was in hell. Grabbing his suitcase, he followed Carol Anne through the crowd, past shops and doors and along the corridor toward the security office.

Fifteen minutes later a five-borough missing persons alarm went out over the police radio: "Nine year old African boy, about four feet two inches tall, wearing grey suit. Answers to name of Tsepo. Speaks basic English, but is from Lesotho, Africa. Report any information to 8th Precinct."

The young officer at the desk looked at Father Alberto and Carol Anne. "Does he speak Lesotho too?" he asked.

"Sotho," corrected Carol Anne.

"Sotho," the officer repeated with a blank look. "Well, that's all I can do for now."

"But can't you—can't we—" Father Alberto stood helplessly in front of the desk.

"You can contact us in the coffee shop," Carol Anne said to the officer. She took Father Alberto's arm and led him out into the hallway. "Children get lost all the time in New York," she lied. "But we'll find him somehow, or someone will. He can't have just disappeared into thin air.

Come on, we'll have a cup of coffee and I'll tell you about Jannie."

Tsepo ran for two blocks without looking back and then glanced over his shoulder to see how fast she was following him. To his surprise and great relief, the sidewalk was entirely empty except for a woman pushing a baby stroller in the other direction. He ducked in between two parked cars, fumbling with the buttons on his fly, and within seconds had left a long stream that ran steadily downhill alongside the curb. Afterward, while he buttoned his pants, he leaned against a fender and closed his eyes, trying to catch his breath and to recover from the two-hour strain on his bladder. He felt so much better that the reality of his situation wasn't apparent to him. He wasn't even thinking of where to go next or what to do. All he felt was relief.

He looked across the street. There was a park. The trees, their bare branches outlined against the early evening sky, provided something familiar in the city landscape. Tsepo crossed the street and walked slowly along the sidewalk outside the park. Toward the end of the block some teenage boys were playing basketball, jumping and shouting and laughing a lot. When he was opposite the basketball court, Tsepo stopped and hooked his fingers into the fence, fascinated by the game and the accuracy of the players. Then someone missed the ball and it bounced against the fence, almost hitting his face. Frightened,

Tsepo jumped back and walked away quickly. At the next corner he turned right onto a crowded avenue with wide sidewalks, and just kept walking. He had absolutely no idea of what else to do.

He walked until it was quite dark and the streetlights came on. These and the lights from the stores made a confusing kind of daylight to Tsepo, one full of unexpected shadows and strange reflections. After a while he felt stunned. Then it began to rain, a steady, windy drizzle. Around him people struggled with umbrellas, bumped each other, sped across streets as cars bore down on them threateningly. Tsepo kept close to the buildings, trying without success to keep from getting wet. Several times he stepped into puddles he couldn't see, for the repetition of the bright lights of the stores confused and misled him. Soon his sneakers were soaked, and dirty too as Cash had promised. His head was wet and even through the heavy suit the dampness had settled onto his shoulders.

He stopped walking and leaned against a doorway. By this time he was so hungry that he felt faint. He put his hand in his pocket and fingered the lollipop. But it's for Jannie, he thought, I don't want to eat it. Behind him someone opened the door. Tsepo jumped away from the doorway and ran down the street.

There seemed to be food for sale in every other store that he passed. He remembered suddenly the rand note that Mama Joy had stuffed into his pocket, and felt much better. He stopped in front of the next restaurant he came to, where hamburgers were being cooked in the window. Tsepo gazed in at the even rows of sizzling meat, while he felt for the rand note to be sure it was still there. Then he pulled open a heavy glass door and went inside.

The store was warm and smelled overpoweringly of meat and onions. Tsepo climbed onto a stool and waited, watching the chef, who was sweating over his grill. "What'll it be?" he asked, wiping the counter with a greasy cloth.

Tsepo hesitated, then pointed to a sign that showed a hamburger and a glass of Coca-Cola. The chef glanced at the sign. "Burger and a Coke," he said, as if he were giving himself the order. "With or without?"

Tsepo stared and shook his head. He didn't understand.

"One burger without," said the chef loudly. "OK, it'll be done in a minute.' With practiced motions he turned all the hamburgers on the grill. Then, pulling a chrome handle, he filled a glass from a red cooler beside him. Then he opened a bun and deftly slid a hamburger inside and pushed the whole thing onto a plate at the same time. Tsepo watched, fascinated. He was almost drooling.

"Here you go. That's 75¢." The chef slid the plate and glass toward him over the counter. Tsepo reached into his pocket and handed across the rand note, then immediately picked up the hamburger and opened his mouth. Just as he was about to bite into it, a hand grabbed his wrist. "This ain't real money," the chef said. "What're you tryin' to pull?"

Tsepo winced and dropped the hamburger onto the plate.

"You want me to call the cops?"

Tsepo wasn't sure what it all meant, but he felt very frightened. He cast a last hungry glance at the hamburger and with one motion wrenched his hand away and slid off the stool. Then he pushed open the heavy door and ran straight across the broad slippery avenue, narrowly missing the traffic that bore down on him. He ran on, ducking around people and parking meters, until he was just too tired and out of breath to run anymore.

He slowed to a walk, but at each step the lights reflected on the glistening sidewalk seemed to assault his eyes, and he had to close them. He tripped and stumbled into a stairwell in front of an all night laundromat, then caught himself on the railing and looked down. It was dark in the stairwell, but warm. A few feet below him an exhaust pipe emitted a steady blast of warm, moist air. Tsepo walked the rest of the way down, then curled up inside his jacket close to the warm pipe. He felt much better lying down, but he was still very aware of the sounds from the street above him. He pulled the ketie out of his pocket for protection, and fell asleep.

About fifteen blocks further downtown, at the 28th Precinct, Father Alberto sat hunched over on a hard wooden bench, staring sleepily at the floor. When a phone rang at the desk across the room, he sat up, blinking.

"Uh-huh," said the desk sergeant. "Um, uh-uh, no." He hung up and glanced across the room at Father Alberto with an apologetic smile. "No, no news, I'm sorry." Then he went back to his papers.

Father Alberto looked down at the floor again and closed his eyes. If he hadn't been so impatient and had gone with Tsepo to the bathroom, none of this would have happened. He had never felt so much at fault in his life.

Eight floors above Manhattan's East River, in her chair beside Jannie's bed, Carol Anne stirred and opened one eye. The first grey light of day showed at the window. The night nurse was making her rounds before going off duty. Only half awake, Carol Anne watched her without speaking. The nurse checked the intravenous drip, checked Jannie's pulse, and then went out, her rubber soles squeaking slightly on the hard linoleum surface of the hall.

Uptown, a driver backed up his green sanitation truck onto the sidewalk so that its rear loading platform was as close to the buildings as possible. At 6:00 A.M. the traffic was light and the street still fairly deserted, with only a few people hurrying to or from work. It was cold out, and their bodies were all bent slightly, as if to hold in a circle of warmth they had brought with them. The loader pulled his hat down over his eyes, slipped on his thick dirty canvas gloves, and walked down the laundromat stairwell. He was almost all the way down before he noticed Tsepo. He dropped to his knees and reached out to shake the boy awake. "Hey kid—wake up! What are you doing here? Come on—wake up!"

Tsepo opened his eyes, expecting his mother and unable to remember where he was or why. He looked at the loader, but then closed his eyes again. The driver, noticing some interruption in their schedule, jumped down from the truck and looked over the railing.

"It's a kid. He looks frozen," the loader said. "Hey kid—wake up!" He shook Tsepo again. Tsepo's eyes flew open. Terrified, he scrambled to his feet and ran up the stairwell and then out into the avenue.

"Probably ran away from home," said the driver, as they watched him disappear into the next street. He picked up Tsepo's ketie, which had fallen to the ground. "What's this?"

Taking it from him and turning it over, the loader shrugged. "Some kind of a slingshot, ain't it?" He threw it into the back of the truck and reached for the garbage cans.

Tsepo sat down on a stone stoop to catch his breath. The sleep had refreshed him but he was ravenous, for by this time he hadn't eaten for a day and a half. His normally round belly felt concave, and his pants drooped. He took the lollipop out of his pocket and stared at it for a while. Jannie would certainly understand, he decided, so he unwrapped it and licked it thoughtfully for a few minutes. Then with a sigh he rewrapped it. He knew that even if he ate it all up he would still need more food.

It was too cold to sit still for very long. He got up and walked slowly down the street, thinking that perhaps he might be able to find some food, or catch an animal to eat, as one could in Nohateng. But though he looked with a careful eye, the only animals he saw were an occasional cat, dogs being walked strangely on leashes, and pigeons. He decided to try for the last kind if he could catch one. At the end of the street was a small fenced off square of cement with a basketball hoop mounted at the back. Wandering among the lines and circles painted on the asphalt was a flock of pigeons. Tsepo stalked them carefully, keeping in back so they wouldn't see him. When he had reached a good point, he put his hand in his pocket for the ketie, and realized as he did that he had left it in the stairwell. Quickly he made a dash for the flock, to try to catch one barehanded. But they all flew away. He stood, alone and empty handed in the little playground, feeling worse than ever. First the box confiscated and now the ketie lost. He wanted to cry.

But crying wouldn't help his stomach, he knew that. He left the playground and trudged on, turning a corner into another wide avenue lined with stores, like the one he'd walked along the night before. Most of the stores were still closed, their interiors dark and mysterious behind drawn locked gates. But in the middle of the block a coffee shop was open. Behind the steamy windows Tsepo could see it had one long counter and was crowded with people. He stood just outside the door, trying to decide whether to go in.

A man came up behind him, and reaching over Tsepo's head, opened the door. Tsepo sneaked under his arm just as the door was closing, and found himself upon entering almost underneath a broad black marble counter. Stepping back, he saw an array of baked goods lined up in boxes— donuts, crullers, rolls, pastries. His mouth watered and his stomach contracted painfully.

There were two men wearing white aprons behind the counter, both working nonstop, pouring coffee, grabbing pastries with metal tongs, taking money, and making change. Tsepo edged up to the counter and waited until he was sure no one was looking at him. Then he grabbed two donuts and dashed outside, using his whole body to shove open the door. Unfortunately he ran right into the stomach of a big fat man who was on his way in. "Hey, watch it!" the man yelled.

One of the men behind the counter noticed the scene in the doorway. "Hold it right there!" he shouted, and lifting up one corner of the counter he dashed to the door, his white apron flapping around his legs like a skirt. He had been troubled by kids stealing lately and wanted to put a stop to it right away.

But Tsepo had squirmed through, under the elbow of the fat man, and was running down the street, taking large bites of donut as he ran. He turned a corner, ducked into a doorway, and crouched behind a garbage can.

Cursing furiously and puffing hard, the store owner came around the corner. "Stop—you damn kid! *Wena ngani—ima!*"

Tsepo was so startled by these last words that he stood up, knocking over the garbage can. The man made a dash for him and grabbed him by the collar. "What the hell do you think you're doing? I'm tired of you kids stealing from me!"

"*Ke lapile!*" Tsepo begged. "I'm hungry—*ke lapile!*" He tried to pull away.

But the man kept hold of him, staring at him in amazement. Tsepo's shirt buttons had come undone, revealing the goat's horn on its leather thong. Still holding him by the collar, the man lifted the horn. "*Helang! Na u-u buoa sesotho?*"

The man had asked if he were speaking Sotho. Slowly Tsepo nodded.

"*Fatseng la Amerika?*"

Tsepo gulped, finding it hard to keep back the tears. "I c-came to see Jannie," he began, but . . . *lah . . lahlehile . . .* I'm lost—"

His anger completely forgotten, the store owner gathered Tsepo into his arms. "*Jannie o ile a tsoa,*" Tsepo sobbed, and went on in Sotho, telling the man the rest of his story. Midway, the man picked him up and carried him around the corner into the warmth of the store.

"Draw me a cup of hot chocolate," he said to his startled partner, "and then call Sergeant Smith at the 28th Precinct. You won't believe this, but we've got a lost *African* kid on our hands."

10

When the taxi pulled up the wide driveway to the hospital visitors' entrance, Carol Anne was waiting for them, a vague shape behind the plate glass doors of the lobby. She ran outside and hugged Tsepo so hard that he yelled. "I'm too full to be squeezed," he giggled. Uptown in the coffee shop they had fed him bacon and eggs and toast and jam and milk and cake until he had at last had to push the plate away. The store owners had made a big fuss over him, and people had asked kind questions. He had told them about his lost hamburger and they were sympathetic, and they laughed about the ketie. Some of them even knew what it was. Tsepo had a great time.

Father Alberto finished paying the driver and

followed them in through the revolving door, which Tsepo thought a most remarkable apparatus and insisted on going through twice. When he came out Father Alberto seized his hand firmly. "No more accidents, *please*," he said.

Carol Anne looked at him with sympathy. The strain was beginning to show. "Did the police finally find Tsepo?" she asked.

Father Alberto shook his head. "No, a store owner did. You won't believe this, but he's a Zulu from South Africa, living right here in the middle of New York. Tsepo tried to take some donuts from his store and..."

"I was hungry," Tsepo explained.

"Poor dear," said Carol Anne.

The elevator door opened and they stepped in. Tsepo huddled against Father Alberto, feeling as though he would lose his stomach on the way. "Ooooo," he said, "I think next time I will walk."

In the corridor they met Dr. Martens, Dr. Stanton, and Dr. Benson, who led them down to Jannie's room and quietly opened the door. Morning sun streamed in through the window, and the room felt warm and cheerful. Carol Anne had hung mobiles from the ceiling and bright pictures on the walls, hoping to awaken Jannie by attracting his attention, but her technique hadn't worked. The colorful room provided only more contrast to the pale, inert figure in the bed, enclosed in an oxygen tent and with the intravenous bottle dripping its contents slowly through the yellow tube into his arm.

Tsepo gazed at Jannie, shocked by the apparatus and appalled at the tiny figure behind the plastic tent, shrunken and so different from the boy who had climbed into the tire, even from the broken person they had pulled out of the river below the cliffs.

Dr. Martens stepped to the bed and rolled back the tent, then turned to Tsepo. "Why don't you try talking to him?" he suggested.

Tsepo hesitated, afraid something might happen to the boy in the bed if they even continued to stare at him.

"Don't be afraid," said Dr. Stanton encouragingly.

"We're counting on you to help," Dr. Benson added.

Tsepo walked to the bed. Leaning over, he could barely manage to reach up to whisper in Jannie's ear. "Jannie," he said softly. "Jannie. It's me, Tsepo. I'm here."

Nothing happened. The pale boy didn't move. Tsepo looked at the doctors. "Try again," Dr. Stanton said kindly. "And climb up. He may not be able to hear you." He cranked the bed so that it tilted a little closer to Tsepo.

Tsepo climbed on the bed, so close he thought he could hear the liquid from the bottle dripping into Jannie's arm. "Jannie," he said again, this time louder. "It's me, Tsepo. You were calling me, so I came."

There was still no reaction from Jannie. Tsepo began to feel anxious. He could sense concerned movement behind him from the doctors at the foot of the bed, and he didn't know what to say. He reached for Jannie's hand. "Wake up, please Jannie," he said urgently, squeezing the limp fingers below the cast.

Jannie twitched slightly. There was a noticeable quick movement behind his eyelids, and then slowly, very slowly, he opened his eyes. With difficulty, he tried to focus, but he saw only a moving blur at the foot of the bed.

"Jannie, Tsepo's here," a voice said. "Beside you. Turn around."

Jannie felt the hand in his and turned his head in that direction. When he saw Tsepo his eyes filled with tears, and he began to tremble. "In the tire," he whispered, trying to lift his arm. But the arm in its heavy cast fell back on the blanket and his eyes closed again.

"Father Alberto got you out of the tire," Tsepo said. "Wait Jannie—don't go to sleep again. I brought you something." He reached into his pocket and brought out the lollipop. Though diminished in size, it was still recognizable. "Look Jannie," he said. "Open your eyes. I brought it for you all the way from Nohateng."

Jannie opened his eyes. There was a rustle of delight from the starched coats at the foot of the bed. "Sugar Ball—*o teng?*" he whispered.

Father Alberto walked around and put his face up close to Tsepo's so that Jannie could see him. "Sugar Ball is all right Jannie," he said. "He's protecting Sister Theresa at the mission."

152

Tsepo and Carol Anne giggled at this. At the sight of Father Alberto, Jannie's eyes grew even brighter, and he lay looking at them both with a faint smile on his face.

Father Alberto looked at the blur of white coats through his tears. "You see Doctors? He's already smiling," he said loudly to mask his emotion. "Now that we're here, nothing is going to keep him from getting better." He turned to Jannie. "Right?"

Jannie managed a slight nod. Then Father Alberto helped Tsepo off the bed, Dr. Martens repositioned the oxygen tent, and they all filed quietly out the door.

Outside a nurse was waiting in the hall for Father Alberto. "Someone to see you, Father, in the waiting room," she said.

Father Alberto stared at her, a bit confused. "Me?" He couldn't imagine who it might be.

"I'll come along with you," Carol Anne said. "The doctors want to buy Tsepo a treat in the canteen."

They walked down the long green corridor to the waiting room. Father Alberto dragged his feet. He wanted to say something to her, to tell her how grateful he was to her for saving Jannie's life. But he didn't seem able to talk.

In the sunny waiting room a short plump man with a clerical collar under his overcoat was sitting on a bench reading a magazine. A large camera lay on the seat beside him. He jumped up when they came into the room. "I'm Father

Duggan from the New York Diocese," he said cheerfully, pumping Father Alberto's hand.

"How do you do," said Father Alberto, polite but reserved. "This is Carol Anne Duxley."

"How do you do, Miss Duxley."

"What can we do for you?" asked Father Alberto, after a moment's silence.

"What we'll be wanting is a photo of you and the child," Father Duggan said shyly, indicating the camera. "I've already written the story," he added modestly.

"But what for?" asked Carol Anne.

"For the paper of course—the *Catholic Herald*."

Father Alberto hesitated. The South African radio and newspapers had played up the story enough so that there would surely be some question about Jannie's presence in Nohateng and about his religion. He had to make things clear at once. He said, with a hint of regret: "I'm sorry, Father Duggan, it's just not possible."

Father Duggan frowned, a little puzzled. "But why, Father?"

Father Alberto sighed. "The child is not a Catholic," he said.

Stunned, Father Duggan opened and closed his mouth and then opened it again. "But Father," he said. "I don't under—"

"I'm sorry," Father Alberto said. He went to the door, opened it, and bowed.

Father Duggan picked up his camera and edged toward the door. "But Father," he tried again.

"I'm really very sorry," Father Alberto said firmly, and shut the door in the startled Father Duggan's face.

Once the door was shut his firm facade vanished. Gripping the knob for support, he leaned his head against the door and closed his eyes. He felt exhausted. So much had happened, and he was more than a little confused.

Several weeks later a window in the therapy room was open. The warm breeze carried with it smells of earth and green things growing. It was the first week in April, and everyone had spring fever. Carol Anne looked out the window, which overlooked the hospital lawn. Two employees in white jackets were sitting on a concrete wall, swinging their legs and drinking something out of paper cups. Suddenly one white jacket put down his cup and seized the other white jacket in a long ardent embrace. Embarrassed, but delighted, Carol Anne turned away.

Across the room Jannie was getting his strength back under the supervision of the therapy nurse. He stood within a lane defined by two metal guardrails and was holding on tight with both hands. "OK, now let's see you walk all the way down the lane," the nurse said.

"I can't go that far," Jannie said promptly.

"Well, you couldn't yesterday," said the nurse, "but today you might. Just try."

At the end of the lane Tsepo shouted encouragement. "If you can get to me, I'll give you some of this," he called, waving something in the air.

"What is it?" Jannie asked.

"I can't say," said Tsepo mysteriously. "It might be *mampharoane*."

Jannie giggled and began to walk toward Tsepo.

Father Alberto laughed too. He was sitting on the radiator next to Carol Anne, dressed in his old khaki pants. "You should have seen that Customs inspector's face when he opened Tsepo's box," he said. "There're probably *mampharoane* all over Kennedy Airport by now. I don't think we caught them all."

"Ugh!" Carol Anne said, but she laughed anyway.

Every day Jannie walked longer distances, traipsing back and forth between the guardrails with Tsepo at his side. When the casts were taken off his arms, he skipped rope to strengthen them and practiced on a chinning bar. Soon he was allowed outdoors: first to the hospital courtyard and then to go exploring with the others, who were having a good time "discovering" New York. They strolled down Fifth Avenue all the way to Washington Square, and took the subway all the way to the aquarium in Coney Island. To the children's everlasting boredom, Father Alberto insisted on stopping at every bookshop he could find. They much preferred going with Carol Anne to Army surplus stores. In Central Park they rode the merry-go-round and fed peanuts to the monkeys in the zoo. The sign said the monkeys were from Africa. "We're from Africa too," said Tsepo to the keeper.

"Really? Are there monkeys where you live?"

"Not one," said Jannie. "Cobras, though, goats and cattle and rock dassies."

"And don't forget the *mampharoane,*" said Carol Anne sarcastically.

The keeper hadn't ever heard of *mampharoane.* "Where are you from?" he asked.

"Lesotho," said Father Alberto.

The keeper looked blank. "Never heard of it," he said.

"It's the back of the world," said Carol Anne with a grin, and waving goodbye, they walked on, the four of them as usual hand in hand and blocking the sidewalks.

A week before going home, they got up early one morning to take a ride on the Staten Island ferry. It was raining slightly, and Jannie and Tsepo were disappointed, for they had counted on seeing the ships and the skyline. But they decided to go anyway, and when they came up out of the subway the rain had stopped, although a fine mist remained. From time to time the sun broke through and it was very warm, almost hot. The children ran ahead through Battery Park. They climbed the large steel sculptures and tested each swing in the playground, but they liked best the large binoculars that had little windows to squint through and faced the sea.

A week later Dr. Benson set a small bottle of white pills on Jannie's bedside table. The label on the bottle said URGENT. Beside the table stood a stack of cardboard cartons, one of which was marked KEEP AWAY FROM HEAT—HYDRO-CORTISONE.

Everyone was sitting around on chairs and on luggage amid banners and plastic shopping bags full of souvenirs. They were all talking loudly and drinking a goodbye drink from little paper cups. There were doctors, nurses, physical therapists, technicians, aides. Father Alberto had his eye on a bottle he intended to bring home for Cash. Jannie and Tsepo, dressed alike in new western jackets, jeans, and cowboy boots, were chasing each other around the bed.

"Hey, young man, come here," Dr. Benson called from beside the table. Jannie and Tsepo went to him. He had the small bottle in his hand. "These are your replacement tablets," he said. *Every day* without fail you must take two. Got that?"

Jannie nodded. Then he grinned at the doctor and stuck both thumbs in his western style studded leather belt. "OK pardner," he said.

Dr. Benson smiled. "Good luck, John Wayne," he said. "And remember—keep warm."

Jannie nodded again, very seriously, and Tsepo nodded too.

11

When their homecoming was announced in the
Pretoria paper, Mevroew Pienaar phoned Dominee Wessels, her minister. "They're coming home
Wednesday," she said. "I'd like to be in Nohateng
then. Will you drive me?"

"Certainly," he agreed. She had told him the
whole story, and he was eager to help her rescue
her grandson from the "deprived" and "obviously
dangerous" life he'd been living. It was Dominee
Wessels' intent to take Jannie to Pretoria
immediately, where he could resume his "legiti-
mate" life.

In Nohateng the plane dropped the same paper
in the weekly plastic mail packet. Cash General
picked it up, and driving with one hand, the paper

propped against the windshield, he read the whole story on his way home.

He burst into the store and tossed the packet at Mama Joy. "Look—on the front page!" he yelled. "A picture—and it says they're coming home Wednesday. That's tomorrow! How come they didn't let us know?"

Mama Joy was searching among the letters. "Here's a cable from them," she said, tearing at the envelope.

Cash grabbed it.

MEET US NEXT WEDNESDAY AIRSTRIP 2 P.M. STOP LOVE TO ALL STOP FATHER ALBERTO

Mama Joy snatched the cable back and ran out of the store.

"Where are you going?" he called after her.

"To tell Sister Theresa—*sehole!* And we'll have to have a party for them, right?"

The bell jangled as the door slammed behind her. Chuckling, Cash General went to the third shelf and looked for the bottle in back of the meal sack. It was only one third full. That'll do for tomorrow, he said to himself. But I'll get a new one next Friday in Maseru. I'm sure Father Alberto will have lots of stories about New York!

The next day Jannie, sitting between Cash General's legs, blew the truck horn most of the way home. Squeezed together on the seat next to Cash were Tsepo, with Sugar Ball squirming in his lap, Carol Anne, and Father Alberto, who kept ducking out the window, inhaling fresh air, and then pulling his head back in again. All of them were talking at once. Sugar Ball kept whining and licking Tsepo's face, as though he were washing off whatever Tsepo had acquired in New York. Behind them, lashed haphazardly to the back of the truck, was a jumble of suitcases, boxes, and plastic bags.

In the mission kitchen Sister Theresa heard the horn from two miles off. "They're coming!" she whispered aloud. "They're almost here." She dried her hands and ran to the study, where she took a quick look around to see that everything was in order. Despite everything she felt excited about their arrival, although of course she was worried sick about what would happen afterward. She glanced out the window at the car with the South African license plates and felt dizzy, torn between excitement and fear, while the sound of the horn grew louder.

But they were going to have the homecoming party come "hell" or high water, she decided. Taking a deep breath, she forced herself to relax, and quietly shut the door to the chapel, so as not to disturb those who were waiting there. She went out onto the porch just as the truck pulled into the yard. It was followed closely by a gang of shouting children, who converged on it the moment it stopped. Sugar Ball leaped out of the window, barking loudly. Then a large group of older people, who had been waiting at the store with Mama Joy, came flying across the road and gathered around those who were already gathered around the truck. It was a very noisy scene.

161

Sister Theresa picked up her skirts and ran pell-mell into the crowd, pushing her way until she had gotten to the truck. Cash General handed Jannie out to her and she hugged him ecstatically. Then she set him down and held him at arm's length. "Ah, let's look at you child. Why, you look just fine!" She beamed at him.

Jannie beamed back. He was glad to see her, he had to admit.

Tsepo slid down from the truck and stood grinning at her.

"Tsepo! You've been all the way to New York!" She gave him a big squeeze too. She seemed a very different Sister Theresa, not like her usual self at all.

Father Alberto and Carol Anne were laughing and joking with Cash General and Mama Joy on the other side of the truck. When Sister Theresa walked around to find them, she was aware instantly of their closeness, but for once in her life she felt forgiving. "Welcome home, Father," she said gently, "—and you too, Carol Anne."

"Thank you, Sister," Carol Anne said. Touched by the greeting, she leaned down and planted a kiss on Sister Theresa's cheek. Father Alberto smiled and shook her hand warmly, aware that she seemed changed, but amid all the confusion, he wasn't sure how.

In a few minutes the store was in an uproar. Sister Theresa cut the cake, Mama Joy poured lemonade, and Cash General ladled out ginger beer from an earthenware crock. Every single person in the whole room was talking. Tsepo boasted in Sotho about all the places they'd visited and everything that went on in New York. "*Hele! He le e so bone—Fifth Avenue—le television—*"

"Television *keng*?" someone asked.

"*Sehole*!" Tsepo replied. "Of course, television! But *le* zoo! *Le* Coney Island!" With each statement went a complete description, but then Father Alberto began to tell about the airport and no one was listening to Tsepo anymore. Suddenly he remembered the koloi he had made as a present for Jannie. He gave Jannie a look, and they snuck outdoors.

When she saw that the children had gone, Sister Theresa pulled Father Alberto aside, trying to whisper something in his ear. She appeared tense and suddenly upset. But he couldn't hear her at all. "Let's go to the mission," he said, and after saying goodbye to Cash General and Mama Joy, they crossed the road. "Now what is it, Sister?" he asked, as they went up the stairs and into the hall.

"Come into the study, Father," she whispered. "I—I have something to—to tell you." She shut the door behind them quietly, trying to get up enough courage to tell him the news.

He hadn't seen the South African car parked out in back. Father Alberto looked at her curiously. "What is it, Sister?" he asked again, resigned to offering explanations.

"There's someone here to see you," she began.

"To see me?" Father Alberto's voice rose. Nervously he waited for her to continue.

"In there," she said in a low voice, indicating the chapel.

"Who?" Father Alberto whispered, afraid of who it might actually be—the Archbishop, or Steve Mawanga...

"A...a woman who claims she's Jannie's grandmother," she whispered back. "And her minister has come too."

Father Alberto felt cold all over, through to his bones. He looked at the floor.

Sister Theresa swallowed hard, trying to remain calm. "Father, I have a...a confession to make."

Father Alberto sat down at his desk. He was so stunned that he mumbled, "What do you wish to confess, Sister," automatically, as though they were in a confessional a thousand miles away.

"I...I told them...I told them the child was ours," she said.

For a moment Father Alberto looked at her as though she were not aware of her mistake. "But Sister, the child *is* ours," he said.

"No Father, you don't understand," she said firmly, anxious to make it clear so she could get it off her chest. "I told them Jannie was *ours*... yours and mine."

Father Alberto's eyes widened. "*You* told them *that*?" He stared at her, unable to believe that

Sister Theresa Marguerita of Belfast would ever compromise herself so. She would not meet his gaze, but stood in front of the door to the chapel, looking over his head at the crucifix. The look on her face was that of a desperate woman who would do anything to fight for her child.

Father Alberto sighed. He would have liked to join her, but he knew that, after all, he was the one who was wrong. "Sister, open the door," he said quietly. She put her hand on the doorknob but she was so frightened that she was unable to turn it. "Open the door—please, Sister," he said again, still kindly, and then she went limp. Father Alberto crossed in front of her, and opening the door, strolled down the aisle of the little chapel toward the people in the front pew. Sister Theresa followed him, head down and mute. She closed the door behind her and stood in front of it, fingering her rosary.

Mevroew Pienaar turned and stood up when they came in. Her grey hair, drawn back into a tight bun, and her old-fashioned black dress gave her the appearance of someone from another era. She was holding a Bible, and though her lined face reflected years of strain, there was a certain peace and calmness in her eyes. The man beside her came up the aisle. "Father Alberto? I am Dominee Wessels, Minister of the Dutch Reformed Church, Pretoria-Wes."

"How do you do," said Father Alberto, extending his hand.

"And this," Dominee Wessels indicated the woman, "is Mevroew Magdalena Pienaar, a member of my congregation."

Mevroew Pienaar bowed her head courteously at Father Alberto.

There was an awkward silence. "I believe you know why we are here," said Dominee Wessels finally.

Father Alberto nodded. "Yes, but—"

"Permit me to explain then," said Dominee Wessels. He was formal and businesslike, very self-assured. He appeared to be used to having his own way.

The two men sat down in a pew, but Mevroew Pienaar remained standing, looking out the chapel window. "Mevroew Pienaar is a widow," Dominee Wessels began. "She had only one child, a son named Andries, who was married in 1961 to Anna Prinsloo. A few years after their marriage, they moved to Kimberley. He was a digger—"

Father Alberto listened, watching Mevroew Pienaar, whose attention was focused on something outside. "In August, 1968, Andries and Anna disappeared on their way from Kimberley to Durban, with an old woman servant and their young son, who was then about three." Father Alberto remembered the old woman he had buried, and felt he had known this story for a long, long time. "For many years, Mevroew Pienaar searched for them, but—nothing. Until the newspaper. Mevroew?"

There was no answer. She didn't hear him because she was watching Jannie and Tsepo, who had brought the koloi from the tractor shed and were taking it out front to play. In the fall sunshine the wire cart gleamed, its tin can wheels casting bright patterns on the wall. Jannie liked it, but turning to thank Tsepo, he became conscious of someone staring at him and aware of a shape behind the chapel window above him. He stopped, facing the window, and shielded his eyes from the sun so he could see who it was. For a moment he stared at the woman, whose face seemed so familiar. He kept staring, disturbed and puzzled, until he heard Tsepo calling him urgently. Then he dashed off around the corner, pushing Sugar Ball in the little koloi, and stopped dead at the sight of the South African car.

"Mevroew? Mevroew—*die koerant!*" Dominee Wessels was saying.

From her Bible Mevroew Pienaar produced a newspaper clipping: *Die Transvaler's* picture of Jannie and the story of "Mercy Maseru." Her eyes were bright when she handed the well worn clipping to Father Alberto.

"It was only when this picture appeared that Mevroew Pienaar knew her grandson was alive," said Dominee Wessels emphatically, as if the facts were now proved.

But Father Alberto was not about to give in so easily. He waved the clipping at Dominee Wessels. "But with respect, Dominee," he said cautiously, "you have only given me a newspaper clipping that everyone in South Africa has seen. What real proof do you have?"

Dominee Wessels turned. "*Die foto,* Mevroew," he said.

From her Bible Mevroew Pienaar produced another photograph. Dominee Wessels placed it carefully beside the newspaper clipping. The photos were identical. Father Alberto gazed at the new one with interest. It was surely a photo of Jannie, but he had never seen it before. "Where did you get this picture of Jannie?" he asked curiously.

"*Die nie Jannie nie—dis sy pa!*" the woman said quickly. "It's a picture of his father."

In the back of the room Sister Theresa turned pale and clung to the study door. She felt totally shattered

The outside door of the chapel was slightly ajar. Quietly pushing it further open, Jannie and Tsepo crept in and hid behind the confessional, listening.

Father Alberto looked up from the pictures at the cold, self-assured eye of Dominee Wessels. "And if Jannie is indeed Mevroew Pienaar's grandson?" he asked. "What will you do then?"

"By birth and right he is ours," said Dominee Wessels. "He belongs to us, to our church. And as such we want him back."

Sister Theresa came down the aisle. "You mean you want to take him away?" she gasped.

"Of course," said Dominee Wessels. "Since he's ours—"

"But he isn't," Sister Theresa protested weakly. "He's *ours* . . . I mean . . ."

"I understand that you've raised him thus far, Sister," said Dominee Wessels patiently. "But by birth he's an Afrikaner. His birthright cannot be denied."

"But you can't take him away," Sister Theresa said desperately. She was fast becoming hysterical. "You can't take him away, you can't—"

"Sister!" Father Alberto grabbed her by the shoulders and squeezed until she stopped. Still holding her, he turned to Dominee Wessels apologetically. "I think it's time for tea," he said. Then he turned back to Sister Theresa, his eyes pleading for her self-control. "We'll have tea in the study, Sister," he said. "Perhaps Carol Anne will help you."

Pressing her lips together firmly, Sister Theresa nodded at them and left, shutting the study door with a click. At the same moment, at the opposite end of the room, the outside door shut too.

Jannie and Tsepo stumbled outdoors. "They want to take me away," Jannie whispered. "Did you hear them?"

Tsepo just nodded, not knowing what to say or do.

"I've got to hide," said Jannie. "Come with me."

"Where?"

"We'll go over the mountain and hide in the old mine."

"*Che* Jannie, no," Tsepo said. "It's going to be dark soon. Look."

Jannie ignored him. "Hurry. You get a donkey and I'll put Sugar Ball in the generator shed so he won't follow us. I'll meet you at the path." He picked up Sugar Ball and ran around the back.

"Jannie!" Tsepo cried, but he knew that if he refused to go, Jannie would go alone. He turned and ran for the kraal.

Opening the door of the shed, Jannie pushed the dog inside. "Sorry, Sugar," he whispered. Then shutting the door, he locked the padlock and ran around the back of the mission, following Tsepo through the dry fields toward the kraal.

Sister Theresa couldn't find Carol Anne to help her so she managed the tea alone, through a real effort of will. In silence, her hands steady, she poured a cup for Mevroew Pienaar, who accepted it graciously, and then handed another to Dominee Wessels.

Father Alberto smiled at her gratefully, and then began what he hoped would be his justifying argument. "Now Dominee," he said, "as you realize we have grown to love this child as our own, and his happiness is our only concern, as I am sure it is yours."

Everyone nodded agreement. It was hard to disagree with that. "But with respect," Father Alberto continued, "although I would not presume to judge your people or your way of life, Jannie has grown up in a society which is very— different from yours." He hoped he'd been tactful enough.

Dominee Wessels stared at Father Alberto over his teacup. He did not exactly approve of priests in khaki pants or the way of life of integrationists in general.

Father Alberto leaned forward. "Please," he said, "I ask you to consider, as a minister of God, can the child suddenly and without warning be switched from our way of life to yours?"

Dominee Wessels looked hard at Father Alberto. "Father, the love and guidance you have given Jannie is beyond question. But now that we have found him, it's our duty to raise him as one of his people. He can't be denied his heritage, after all."

"But by raising him as one of your people, will he be happy?"

Dominee Wessels had his own ideas about happiness. He set his empty cup on the desk, his mouth turned up in a faintly sarcastic smile. "Happy? Yes, I think so," he said.

Father Alberto knew he had run straight into a hard concrete wall. He thought suddenly of South Africa, its separate schools, stores, even telephone booths for black and white. How could Jannie adjust to all that? He turned to Mevroew Pienaar. "Do you really wish to take Jannie away *now*?" he asked.

Mevroew Pienaar put her cup down, choosing

her words. "*Nee*," she said reflectively, "we must wait...time will teach us..."

With a glance of restrained relief at Father Alberto, Sister Theresa began gathering the cups. At least it wouldn't be today, and perhaps—

"And now, please, may I meet my grandson?" Mevroew Pienaar asked.

Sister Theresa turned to her with a smile. "Of course," she said. "I will fetch him right away."

12

Carol Anne walked slowly and thoughtfully up the mountain path, carrying a plastic bag labeled Hudson's Army Surplus Store. The air felt cool and fresh as she climbed, even chill. It had been something of a shock to find that it was fall going on winter in Nohateng, since she had left in the middle of the summer. Suddenly winded, she sat down to catch her breath, realizing with a shudder after she had sat down that she could see the mountain-that-falls-into-the-sky.

But today the view was peaceful. Below her the mission, the store, the harvested grain fields lay familiar and from this distance, silent, under the afternoon sun. "The back of the world," she said aloud. She looked at the mountains a while and then rested her chin on her knees, thinking.

A sudden blast of cold air made her shiver. Carol Anne sat up and looked out again at the mountains. At the farthest range a storm was brewing, its dark thunderheads rolling up fast. I'd better get going, she thought, and grabbing the bag, hurried up the path.

Rakwaba was pleased to see her and eyed the plastic bag with ill-concealed interest. "Is it for me?" he asked, rather formally.

"Open it and see," said Carol Anne with a grin.

Rakwaba extracted a box and then from some tissue paper inside it a pair of large brown U.S. Army combat boots. His face broadened into an enormous pleased smile. With careful and deliberate motions, he put on first one and then the other, stood up, stomped around, and then sat down again beside Carol Anne.

"Thank you and welcome back to Nohateng," he said, and reached for her hand.

It was the warmth of his gesture that took Carol Anne over the edge. Her eyes filled with tears.

Suddenly, the wind rustled the grass mat in Rakwaba's doorway. With a nervous glance outside, Carol Anne stood up. "There's a storm coming," she said. "I'd better go."

"I will wear your present with pride," Rakwaba said, beaming at his feet.

With a goodbye nod, Carol Anne ducked out through the doorway and started along the path. Halfway down, where she had rested before, she looked out and saw Jannie and Tsepo coming along the narrow road far below. They were riding a donkey, and edging it down the slope toward the river. Behind them, the thunderclouds were clearly visible and coming on fast.

Carol Anne stared at the boys, amazed and furious. "What kind of dumb trick are those kids playing now!" she said angrily, and then ran quickly to tell Father Alberto and Sister Theresa where they were.

The river was higher than normal, swollen because of the rainy season. Jannie was sitting in front, holding the donkey's rope, and Tsepo was behind him, holding onto Jannie's waist. He was trying not to hold on too tight because of Jannie's operation scars. He felt very anxious and averted his head when they passed the rock where Jannie had come down in the tire. Turning, he almost lost his grip.

Jannie was much less afraid of the river than he was of the strangers who were going to take him away. The man, especially, terrified him. He guided the donkey to a shallow place where they could cross and urged him into the water, but the river raged around the animals' legs and he brayed in protest. Jannie threatened, kicked, cajoled— and after a struggle they got across. Tsepo looked back. The sky behind them was completely overcast. "Jannie, let's go back," he said.

But Jannie would not hear of it. On the other side of the river there was an overgrown path that had once been the road to the mine. After the mine turnoff it led indirectly to the higher mountains that lay to the north and west of Nohateng. Jannie urged the donkey up. It was a steep path, and as they climbed it began to rain lightly. Tsepo kept trying to get Jannie to turn around but he wouldn't. "They'll take me away if I go back," he kept saying. Gradually the intermittent rain became a dense grey fog, as the heavy clouds swirled down. Both boys were still wearing their cowboy suits, their homecoming clothes, and soon they were soaking wet.

Neither of them knew the path very well. In the deep mist they passed by the sign that indicated the turnoff to the mine, and instead kept going higher up into the mountains. It was getting darker every minute.

Jannie began to shiver. He felt frightened and alone, even with Tsepo there, because he felt sick. His head drooped over his hunched shoulders. He began to mumble. "Cold," he said. "I'm c-c-co—"

Tsepo changed places with him and took the rope, guiding the donkey slowly along the barely visible path. But as the path got muddy the donkey began to miss its footing; it slipped and slid back as much as it went ahead. Tsepo struggled to keep to the path. It was almost impossible to see anything at all other than the ground beneath them.

Jannie slumped against him. He was shaking all over. Suddenly Tsepo thought of Jannie's pills. He was supposed to take one every day right after tea. "Jannie," he said urgently. Jannie moaned.

Tsepo shook the stiff wet shoulder. "Jannie! You have to take your pills. Let's go home!"

Jannie trembled violently and almost fell off. "Tsepo—I'm so cold," he said in a faint whisper, and then suddenly, as though he had no more strength, he began slipping off the donkey's back. Tsepo grabbed at him, but the donkey moved ahead, and Jannie fell to the ground.

Tsepo jumped off and ran back to him. Jannie lay on the path, curled up and trembling. As Tsepo tried to lift him up, he saw out of the corner of his eye that the donkey was moving away. He let go of Jannie and ran after the donkey. But his quick movements frightened the already tense wet animal, and it bolted away into the darkness. "*Sehole—sehole tooe!*" Tsepo screamed. It would be useless to try to chase it in this fog. They would have to walk. He retraced his steps to Jannie, who had not moved, and tried to lift him up and set him on his feet. But Jannie's shaking knees buckled, and he slid out of Tsepo's arms and tumbled once more to the ground.

Tsepo crouched beside him. Jannie's face looked deathly pale. He was beginning to resemble that other boy, the one in the hospital with a yellow tube into his arm. Tsepo bent down and whispered in his ear, as he had in the hospital: "Jannie, wake up, Jannie, wake up."

There was no answer. Tsepo stood up. His heart was pounding violently, and he felt as frightened as he had been when he was lost in New York. He had no idea where the mine turnoff was, but he knew Jannie was supposed to keep warm. Dr. Benson had said so. He would have to find them some kind of shelter. Desperately, Tsepo grabbed Jannie under the arms and tried to haul him upward, but the heel of his boot caught on a sharp rock and tore. He fell backward, onto the muddy path and Jannie collapsed on top of him. It's too hard, Tsepo thought. I can't, he's too heavy. We'll have to go down. He got to his feet and began to drag Jannie in the other direction. He went down a few feet, stumbled, and went a few feet more. Jannie was by this time a dead weight, only barely conscious, and each time Tsepo stumbled he took Jannie's full weight on his back. He noticed suddenly that he had strayed off the path, and that the ground beneath his feet had become only a jagged and uneven rock ledge. Tsepo stopped, breathing heavily, thinking of the rocky precipice, of the mountain-that-falls-into-the-sky. Where are we? he thought desperately. He still couldn't see more than three feet in front of him.

On his back Jannie stirred. "Cold," he whispered faintly. Twisting, Tsepo grabbed his arms tighter and started off again. "Keep Jannie warm," he said doggedly, "keep Jannie warm—"

But that was as far as he went. On his next step the rocks caught his torn sole. He pitched forward head over heels and rolled, striking his head on a sharp rock. He lost consciousness, and Jannie crumpled into a heap beside him.

Clutching the pill bottle, Sister Theresa hurried down the hall from Jannie's room. Her teeth were clenched painfully tight in her effort to remain calm, but she was as pale as her habit. The front door of the mission stood open, and small groups of people were talking in hushed tones on the porch and out in the courtyard. In the thickening fog the lights from the store appeared faint and distant.

Father Alberto was trying to find some protective clothing for Dominee Wessels at the coatrack when Sister Theresa came down the hall. He handed the minister an old overcoat and then reached for the pill bottle. Sister Theresa handed it to him without a word. When the two men went out onto the porch, she stood watching them for a moment, her fingers reaching for the rosary. Then she quietly shut the door and went into the chapel. Mevroew Pienaar sat in the front pew, her head bowed in prayer.

The tracks of the donkey were still visible. The search party followed them uphill along the meandering path until they disappeared at the place where Carol Anne had seen the boys starting to ford the river. The search party went across on foot over a hastily improvised log bridge, and went up the mountain. Although they carried oil lanterns, it was impossible to really see. From time to time they called the boys' names, but not even an echo came back to them through the swirling mist. They struggled upward and in the increasing darkness eventually reached the turnoff to the mine.

Father Alberto was at the front. "Which way should be go?" he called to Cash General, who was at the rear. Cash came up to him. "Do they know their way to the mine?" he asked.

Father Alberto nodded. "But not very well. We only went there once."

"Maybe they were planning to hide there," said Carol Anne.

"Yes, maybe. It's worth a try." Father Alberto swung his lantern, indicating to the others that they were to turn left.

Red and blue lay in front of Tsepo's eyes, but the colors had no shape, no form. He rolled over on his back. "Jannie," he whispered, but he couldn't even hear his own voice. He struggled to sit up, fell forward, and with great effort began to crawl, searching in the red and blue for a hand, a sign, a part of Jannie.

Suddenly, as though someone had wiped a slate clean, his vision returned, and he could see Jannie lying only a few feet away in some loose sand, under a protruding rock ledge. There was some white stuff on him, and it was only then that Tsepo realized it had begun to snow.

He crawled to Jannie and began digging at the sand, scooping as would a child playing at the beach. Pieces of sharp stone came up with the sand, cutting his fingers, but although he could see very clearly the places where blood stained his fingers, he didn't feel the pain of them at all.

He dug until there was nothing but rock at the bottom of the hole, and then dragged Jannie into it, conscious of certain new sensations in his head, beginnings of red and blue in his eyes. Jannie felt hard. His clothes were frozen stiff. He moaned.

The world began to get large and small and in the corners of his eyes Tsepo saw the color coming fast, like a red and blue sea. "Remember—keep warm," a voice said. Tsepo felt warm himself, only very slow, like a dream. The red and blue were half over his eyes. He took off his boots and put them on Jannie's hands. He took off his shirt and put it over Jannie in the hole. He fell into the hole on top of Jannie and pulled the pile of sand over them. It was warm. He felt pleased as he pulled the warm sand over them and into the warm red and blue tunnel down which he fell.

They had used all the candles in the chapel, Now the last one on the altar had begun to flicker, on the verge of going out. Sister Theresa glanced at the woman in the pew beside her, who was rocking slowly back and forth to the rhythm of her own prayer. "Like I do," Sister Theresa thought, and suddenly felt terribly sorry for this poor woman, sorrier for Mevroew Pienaar than she felt for herself.

There was no other light in the room besides the diminishing candle. Sister Theresa got to her feet, and holding onto the pews, cautiously made her way down the aisle. At the altar she lifted the candle from its holder, and shielding it with her hand, walked step by step out of the chapel and through the pitch dark hallway to the kitchen. When she lit a new candle from the old, light flooded the room. She realized that the house was dark because she hadn't started the generator. She moved the candle closer to the ticking kitchen clock and saw with a start that it was nearly nine o'clock. Nine o'clock—and they weren't back yet! A quick sob escaped her, but then she bit her lip until it hurt to counter the surge of hysteria, and taking the candle, walked carefully out of the kitchen and opened the back door into the generator shed.

Something furry jumped wildly at her legs. Sister Theresa screamed and almost dropped the candle. But the fur had a tongue and whined and she realized that it was Sugar Ball. She tried to let him out the door but it opened a crack and then jammed against the padlock. They must have locked him in, she thought. Wet snow drifted in through the crack. The dog began to bark without stopping and to scratch at the door.

"This way, Sugar Ball," Sister Theresa called to him, and clutching the candle stumbled through the hall to let him out the front door. He scrambled over the frosty porch and disappeared, still barking, from the sound of it on his way up the mountain. He'll find them, she thought, even if no one else has. She stood in the doorway until she could no longer hear him, then wearily retraced her steps to the chapel. There seemed to be no sense to starting the generator. She put the candle into its holder on the altar and sat down once more in the pew. Mevroew Pienaar had not moved.

It was snowing heavily when the search party first heard the dog. "That's Sugar Ball," said Father Alberto. The barking continued.

"He's far away," Carol Anne said.

"Let's go."

Lanterns bobbing in the darkness, they followed the sound, winding their way along the slippery snow-covered path to the higher mountains.

Running the last few yards, Father Alberto got to them first. He saw the snow on Tsepo's bare back, on the still, stiff body. "Oh, God in heaven," he sobbed, and thrusting the lantern into Carol Anne's hands, he fell to his knees and began digging away the sand. Jannie moaned.

The next day was sunny and cold, and no traces of the storm remained. Rakwaba stood looking out over the path and at the mountains beyond. It was so clear that he could see to the last range of the Drakensberg.

Down at the mission a bell was ringing, its regular rhythm evoking a constant and clear pattern in Rakwaba's mind. He squatted and threw the bones once, shook his head, and rose.

Below him on the mountain he could see a long line of people from the village as they went down the path. With slow, measured steps, keeping to the rhythm of the bell, he made his way down and joined them.

Father Alberto was standing at the open grave, staring at the small wooden box at the bottom of it. They had dug the hole too wide and the coffin looked even smaller than it was, and when he looked at it his sorrow became unbearable. But everyone was waiting. Out of the corner of his eye he could see Sister Theresa's fingers working along her rosary. He swallowed hard and then began to read from his missile in an almost inaudible voice: "God, who ordained the services of Angels and men in a wonderful order...." He finished the prayer and stepped back, and then beside him Dominee Wessels came forward.

Rakwaba watched them all—the villagers, Cash General and Mama Joy clinging to each other, Tsepo's mother and father and aged grandmother, their heads bowed in grief, and Carol Anne, who wept softly into her handkerchief. Jannie stood next to his grandmother, looking over the edge of the deep hole. The tears streamed down his face, but he made no attempt to stop them.

Father Alberto took a handful of dirt from the waiting pile and threw it in. "May his soul rest in peace," he murmured. Then catching Rakwaba's eye, he nodded to him.

Rakwaba came forward, shuffling slowly in his heavy boots, for he seemed to have grown older and felt very tired. "Find the *Badimo*, Tsepo," he said simply. "Be spirit of African earth, spirit of sky, and we will know you in *metsa ea lefatse*, the roots of all things." He threw a handful of earth on the coffin and turned away, staring at the mountains.

When everyone had gone, Rakwaba helped Father Alberto shovel the last bit of earth over the grave. "I was going to train him to take my place," he confided suddenly, "since I do not have a son of my own."

Father Alberto looked at him but said nothing. Rakwaba glanced at the car in the courtyard with its South African plates. "You will lose your son too," he said.

Father Alberto straightened up and followed the old man's gaze, watching Mevroew Pienaar and Jannie as they walked slowly across the road. "Yes," he said simply. Rakwaba was probably right. He stopped shoveling and leaned on his spade. "Tsepo told me he believed in Badimo," he said, "after Jannie was hurt. He asked me why God had let such a terrible thing happen."

"What did you tell him?"

Father Alberto shrugged. Then with a sad smile, he asked: "Why did the Badimo let such a terrible thing happen to Tsepo?"

Rakwaba brushed the remaining dirt from his hands. "The same questions trouble all people," he said. "*Mokhoa o mong—tsela di fapane*. The way is the same, only the paths are different." He paused. "We will talk sometime," he said. Then he turned and started slowly along the path toward the mountain.

THE BEST IN FICTION FROM BERKLEY

COMING TO   (K3046 — $1.75)
    by Alan Brody

DEKKER   (D3079 — $1.50)
    by Lou Cameron

WATERS OF DECISION   (K3075 — $1.75)
    by Warren Adler

NASHVILLE LADY   (Z3088 — $1.25)
    by B. C. Hall

TWYLA   (N3076 — 95¢)
    by Pamela Walker

THE SAND CASTLES   (T3130 — $1.95)
    by Louise Montague